PRAISE FOR 'IN

"Chills down my spine... Eerie... I was taken by surprise when I learned the truth."

— OLIVIA TANG, A RAINBOW OF BOOKS

"Had to keep reading. Action packed and tense. Gripping psychological thriller that can mess with your head."

— ALICE AND THE BOOKS

"So delightfully creepy and tragic."

— SOPHIE JULLIPAT POSEY, COMPOSER/WRITER/POET

What would you do if you couldn't remember your own life?
If all you had were fragmented and foggy memories that seemed
out of place?
That's how I'm learning to live. I catch myself questioning
everything and everyone. Every person is a stranger ...even my
own wife and our son.

Just when I think I'll go mad from this, I get glimpses. Visions of
events and people that sometimes seem familiar.
But other times, these apparitions are otherworldly and
threatening. Are these visions just a result of the accident?
Senseless chatter from my damaged brain? Or are they echos of
my real memories?

With every day that passes, I get a growing feeling that
something isn't right. The darkness in my mind plays tricks on
me, as if intentionally. Am I grasping at straws as I lose my
mind? Or is there something more sinister happening?

Things are getting worse now, and it's a race against time to find
out the truth, lest I end up living the rest of my life like this.

Lost.

In the dark.

IN THE DARK

DANIEL FOX

COPPER
CROWN
PUBLISHING

IN THE DARK

Published by Copper Crown Publishing
Editing and Interior Formatting by Elaine York / Allusion Graphics, LLC
www.allusiongraphics.com

Cover Design by Cassy Roop / Pink Ink Designs
www.pinkinkdesigns.com

For Anjee.

...

The first one was always going to be for you.

1

"I'll remember you said that." I use a hint of sarcasm, but I still mean it.

A small giggle escapes her lips. Feathers tickle my forehead for just an instant.

Then nothing. Black. Silent.

My body feels heavy and weighed down. I try to raise my arms, but no matter how hard I try, they simply won't move. I try to speak but nothing comes out. My voice is completely gone. Little patterns of light dance across my closed eyelids, but they won't open. From far away, I can hear distant voices chattering, yet I can't tell what they are saying. Someone is holding my hand. Their skin is smooth and feminine. It's a woman. I smell her perfume. It has a hint of jasmine and this reminds me of her. I miss her. She's whispering now, close. I can almost feel her lips on my ear, her breath soft and warm. "I love you."

More black. More silence.

The noise is so sudden and so loud, I jerk awake with a jolt. Sitting upright, my head is spinning in the darkness. It's so dark in here, yet I do feel a bit relieved because it's no longer the black and dead silence I've been trapped in. The dizziness subsides a little and my eyes are adjusting. For a moment, panic starts to creep in. Where am I? What was that noise? Looking around, I see that I'm in a hospital room. The shades are drawn and flowers sit in vases throughout the room. The TV is on but with no sound. A car commercial is on, the car whizzing up and down the hills on a country road. On the far side of the room, a purple Mylar balloon is moving in the wind of the air conditioning vent, scraping back and forth along the wall, making a little crinkly sound. The balloon has words printed on it, but I can't focus enough to see what it says. There are no clocks in here, so I have no idea what time it is. I feel a chill on my skin and notice how cold it is in here. This room is so quiet that I can hear my own breathing, but nothing else. There is no sign of life other than my own. Surveying my bed, I see that I'm connected to an IV. My head hurts and as I reach up to touch it, I notice that my left hand is wrapped up in a cast down to the middle of my forearm. Using my right hand instead, I feel a bandage on my forehead. My eyes are adjusting more, or maybe the sun is coming up. I'm not sure which, but more details appear. The flowers are mostly roses and carnations, shriveled and dry as if they've been here for a while. Little cards are placed in many of them, though I can't make out what they say either. The car commercial is still on. A young couple smiling at each other in a way that's much too happy and cheesy to be realistic. The TV screen says 'muted' in the bottom corner and I see the controller on the far counter next to a metal sink. My skin itches. Looking down at myself, I'm wearing a blue hospital gown, my body tucked tight into the perfectly folded blankets and sheets, as if I haven't moved an inch. The food tray cart is down by my legs, hanging over the bed, like a sentry awaiting orders. A brown leather coat is draped over it next to a half empty water bottle. In the corner sits a pea-green plastic sofa chair.

Then, I see her.

She's sleeping in the chair. She's maybe in her mid-thirties. She has long blonde hair and is wearing a white t-shirt with a Mercedes emblem on it, lightly snoring. Maybe she can help. I start to speak, to call out to her, but my throat is too dry to allow it. Suddenly overcome with thirst, and without thinking, I reach for the water with my left hand. My left arm sends a jolt of white-hot pain up to my shoulder slicing into my skull. The pain so intense, I manage to find my voice. "Ahh!"

She stirs, sits up, then yells. "Oh my God, you're awake!"

She's coming across the room to me and, for just a moment, I notice her striking grey-blue eyes. Other footsteps rushing down the hall bringing me back to this moment.

"Honey! Can you hear me? " Her voice turns down a level and it stops my head from splitting apart. The nurse comes rushing into the room, her face half-buried under a crazy pile of curly red hair. She seems way too young to be a nurse.

"Mr. Lewis, try to stay calm," she says.

I am calm. It's the blonde who needs calming down. They both start talking at the same time so I can't understand a word from either of them.

"I know you're excited, Lisa, but I need to make sure he's okay first." The blonde stops talking but the nurse doesn't. "Mr. Lewis, can you hear me?"

I attempt to speak, but my throat sticks together again and I end up making a little growling sound before I break into a coughing spasm.

A dry, "Yes....water" is all I can manage.

The blonde spins the top off of the water bottle and hands it to me.

"Tiny sips," says the nurse. "I'll get you some ice chips in a minute."

I want to guzzle down the water....to bathe in it... to stand under a waterfall with my mouth open and let it quench every pore of my soul. I force myself to take a couple of small swallows instead. It's the best water I've ever tasted.

"Yes, I can hear you," I say. "What happened? Why am I here?"

The nurse speaks slowly, as if she thinks I'm having trouble understanding English.

"You've had an episode of sorts, Mr. Lewis. You passed out."

"Please, stop calling me that," I correct her. "Mr. Lewis is my dad. Call me Steve."

She starts over. "Steve."

Unable to contain her excitement for one more minute, the blonde jumps in. "Honey, what's the last thing you remember about Tuesday night?"

I think for a moment. Tuesday night? Then, the panic comes over me in a tidal wave. I can't remember anything about any night. I wrack my brain searching for the last thing I can recall. It isn't last night. It isn't even last week. I can't remember anything, and I don't even know who these people are. I feel a cold shiver run up my spine to the base of my skull, sending goosebumps all over my body. I'm shivering.

"What... What the fuck happened?! " I start to get up.

The IV pulls tight on my right arm, pinching my skin. I attempt to swing my legs off the bed, but they're stuck under the blankets. The nurse darts over and attempts to hold my arms.

"Mr. Lewis. Steve. Calm down," she says.

"Calm down?! What the fuck am I doing here?!" I push her back hard with my good arm and she stumbles away from me, tripping backwards and falling flat on her bottom. I try to pull the blankets off my legs with one hand. It proves to be challenging. Just as I've almost got my legs free, the nurse springs up behind me and does something to my IV. I suddenly feel myself falling back into my pillow. Back into the black again.

Silence.

2

"Easy. Take it easy. Everything is okay. You're okay." I hear her voice fading in. It's soft and sweet. She sounds like she's trying to reassure herself at least as much as she's trying to assure me.

I open my eyes and note that I'm still in the hospital. Daylight streams through the window, causing me to squint, yet I notice that the flowers and the balloon are all gone. Everything's been tidied up. I must have been out all night. The blonde is standing by the bed, gently touching my cheek with her hand. I again note her soft touch, yet I can't connect my feelings to her face and it scares me. I fight the urge to panic again. My eyes are adjusting again, and I see a doctor standing here. A young Asian man holding a clipboard up to his face. He has reading glasses propped up on top of his head.

"Hello, Steve. I'm Dr. Bowen. How are you feeling? Better?" He assumes before I can answer. He can't seem to stop smiling and one of his front teeth is grey, like all the nerves are dead in it, past the point of resurrection, and I find this a bit ironic, so much so that I want to laugh out loud considering his profession is trying to keep people alive.

"I don't feel sick. A littler sore, but...more than anything, I need someone to tell me what the hell happened and what I'm doing here," I say, trying to stay calm. I don't want them to sedate me again.

He smiles his grey tooth smile. I find it strangely comforting, in an odd way. "First of all, medically, you're okay, so please try to stay calm. You passed out in your house three nights ago. Your wife found you on the kitchen floor but she couldn't wake you, so she called for an ambulance. You've been here ever since."

Now I'm starting to feel it again. The fear. "What..." I start, but he interrupts me.

"I know this is really scary, but it's very important that you stay calm so that we can work together to get you home again. You took a nasty fall, causing lacerations on your forehead. You have a small tear in your bicep tendon, and you've fractured your humerus. That is, the bone in your upper forearm. You've also broken your ring finger and fractured your pinky on your left hand. I'm sure this all sounds really bad, but we don't expect any of this to be permanent or cause any permanent symptoms. Our primary concern at this point is what may have caused you to pass out, and why we could not wake you for so long," he says, all in one breath.

Before I can say anything, he continues. "Please don't let this scare you because, again, you are fine. But technically, you've been in a coma for three days. We've run several tests and find nothing irregular. We'd like to keep you for a little while longer to monitor things before we proceed."

I don't know what he means by 'proceed' but I can't stay quiet any longer.

"Doctor, I have no recollection of falling. I don't even remember a house! I can't... I don't..." I feel a swell of guilt in the pit of my stomach as I say it. "I don't recognize this woman." I point to the blonde.

Her eyes fill up before I even get the last word out. One tear escapes and races down her left cheek marking her face with a little wet line. She wipes it quickly, and falls back into the chair. I feel so disconnected from this moment, like I'm not even here. She looks down to her feet, then back up at me. I feel like I can hear the blood rushing through by brain, making a sort of swishing sound in my ears, drowning out everything. I close my eyes for just a moment. Opening them back up, I notice the blonde is still wearing the white Mercedes t-shirt.

What happens next is all a blur. The doctor says something about the injury not being nearly bad enough to cause amnesia. Further testing is in order. Something about seeing a specialist and CAT scan results. She sits there silently, letting me take in all of the information that she's surely heard from the doctor already over the past three days. I'm so scared, and I wonder for a moment if I'm dreaming. Maybe I'll wake up and it'll all be back to normal. I try, unsuccessfully, to imagine what might make me remember. What might feel normal? I search for any part of this situation that might feel normal...something that I can grasp onto like a lifeline to help draw me back to the side of what should be my ordinary life.

Hours go by. The doctor must have left the room at some point. I don't hear him talking anymore, but I vaguely recall saying yes and no in response to his seemingly endless barrage of questions. They took another blood sample and asked me even more questions. These more specifically about what I can and cannot remember. I know my name. I remember being a kid. I remember being an adult. I remember friends, family, and my parents. I remember school and girls. What starts to become more and more apparent is that I can't remember much of anything past college, and I'm drawing a blank for much of that too.

Sitting here in this room with her, I feel the guilt and the panic fighting for control. I can't remember her, yet I do feel a sense of affection deep down that struggles to surface. I also feel a sadness. Lisa. The nursed called her Lisa. She's fallen asleep again. Apparently, she has gotten almost none since we arrived. Really looking at her now, I see that she's pretty. Shoulder-length, dirty-blonde hair. Long, thin legs. But even in her slumber she looks tired. I can see the dark circles under her eyes from here. The nurse tells me that every minute of her time has been spent at my side since the accident. She has refused to leave. I can only imagine what this must be like for her. Thinking about this keeps the fear at bay. Focusing on all of the questions I have about her, and less on the unanswered ones about me, doesn't work for long. I feel it creeping in and again, I'm so scared.

"Hey," I whisper. "Psssst!!" She stirs and then sits upright.

"Steve? Are you okay?" She asks, tears still lingering in her eyes, just waiting for the floodgates to open.

"Well, no. I'm really not. But let's talk," I say. "I.. uhh.. I'm scared," I blurt out.

"Oh, honey. I'm scared too. " She slides the chair over to the bed and grabs my good hand with both of her hands. I smell perfume again. It brings forth an "emotion that I can't nail down, but it's a good one. It's comforting, and I squeeze her hand a little. She squeezes back.

"You really can't remember anything about us?" she asks. This time, no tears and I sense a strength in her, or do I remember that about her? Either way, I like it.

"I'm so, so sorry. I don't," I tell her. Now I feel like I'm going to cry for her.

"Steve, if you don't remember me and you don't remember our life... our family... " she trails off, yet stays solemn. Her face a mask of confusion, attempting to figure out the best way to solve this enigma.

"I'm sure it will come back," I suggest, not being sure of that at all.

"Do you remember Tyler?" she asks.

I pause and focus on the name for what must seem like an eternity. Nothing. "I don't." I say. The tears well up in her eyes again. This time, none of them escape.

"Tyler is our son. He is our son." Now she cries. Silently, but she does. Big crocodile tears drip down onto her shirt and onto the bed. I feel them on my hand, but I can't see them through my own tears. We sit like this for a while, squeezing each other's hand. I don't know how much time has gone by and it doesn't even matter. It's dark again. I slide over to one side of the bed and pull her into it with me. We lie there, side by side, holding hands. Eventually, I hear her softly snoring. I find that familiar... or do I remember it? That doesn't matter either. She just needs some rest.

WE SPEND the next three days in that room. The doctor says I'll have to get an appointment for further testing with a Dr. Lambert, a neurosurgeon who specializes in brain injuries. Lisa comes and goes a few times during these three days. She's become more and more quiet and withdrawn. She's had to run to her mom's to check on Tyler and get some things. I spend my time watching TV shows with titles and actors that I've never heard of, trying to remember anything. The doc tells me not to try too hard, but to let it come naturally. He also surprises me with news that's nothing short of ridiculous. I've been given a clean bill of health and they are going to let me go home. Aside from the gaping hole in my memory, and the unexplainable three-day coma, I'm fine. I almost laugh at the thought.

I say to myself: "Mr. Lewis, you fell for reasons we can't figure out and hit your head hard enough to put you in a coma, but you're good-to-go!" It sounds ludicrous.

I've spent the better part of the day awaiting the final paperwork so that I can go home. Home. Going to a strange place with a woman I don't know and calling it home. I'm more afraid of this than I am of staying here longer. I've grown familiar with this room. It feels more like home than anywhere else, especially where this day's journey will take me, and I'm reluctant to let it go. My repeated asking the doctor and nurses if they are sure I'm okay to go isn't delaying anything, so I stop.

As if on queue, Lisa comes trotting back in with some of my things and a bag of food. Real food. My appetite has been all but non-existent since I woke up, but the smell of the food she brought in is mouth watering. She slides a green backpack off of her shoulder and tosses it in the chair. Turning toward me, I see she's carrying a brown paper bag with woven paper handles.

"It's a steak from Lenny's Chophouse," she says. Opening the paper bag, she sets the plastic carryout plate down on my tray and starts cutting a steak into bite-size pieces. I guess I'm going to have to eat food mostly one-handed for a while, or have someone cut up my food for me, like my mom used to do for me when I was four. How is it that I can remember something that was decades ago, yet can't remember this person sitting in front of me? I hover on that thought for a moment. Being so dependent on a stranger until my memory returns sounds dreadful.

"This one is your favorite," she says. "I ordered extra seasoning on the steak, medium rare with extra blue cheese on the salad, the way you always order it."

The food is delicious. It's absolute perfection, and that scares me. She knows me better than I know me. It makes me realize how dependent I am on her to keep my sanity. I force myself to focus on the food and not the fear. It is delightfully distracting. She grabs the green backpack and starts pulling things from it.

Things she's gotten from home. A change of clothes for me, shoes, a belt, my toothbrush, and a comb. I don't recognize any of it.

Over the past three days, we've talked about Tyler and about her parents. Her father died last year of liver failure. We've been helping her mom a lot since then, and Tyler has spent a lot of time with her mom, too. Especially while I've been in the hospital. Apparently, those two are good for each other.

Tyler. My son. He's four. He hates lasagna. He loves Sponge-Bob, whatever that is. He's intelligent, and doesn't really have friends. Lisa says he's a handful but a loving soul. "An old soul." That's what she calls him. She smiles a lot when she talks about him and the joy in her face is genuine. I find myself looking forward to meeting him—I guess I should say, to seeing him again.

Apparently, Lisa and I met in college and were married soon after. A small wedding with close friends and family. I don't remember any of it, but I do remember college. Little bits of it anyway. University of Wisconsin where I majored in Electrical Engineering. I remember that too. I remember that my own father died soon after my first semester started. He had a massive heart attack. I remember my mother handling it surprisingly well and being more worried about me and how I would take the news and deal with the aftermath. I remember a feeling of unwavering solidarity from my friends, but their faces escape my memory. I remember the support of my girlfriend, or by then was she my fiancé? I can't remember, and I still don't remember her. Not then. Not now. Scanning Lisa's face for even a hint of a memory, she catches me looking at her. She looks back for a moment and I see her grayish blue eyes. They are stunning, and I remember them now. I really do. She smiles briefly, then looks away as if she's afraid to lock my gaze for too long, maybe afraid she'll see my lack of recognition.

She's a stay-at-home mom. We own a painting company together, which I run. I guess engineering wasn't for me after all. I briefly wonder how well I'll run the painting company now. We live in an upper middle-class neighborhood within a few minutes drive to her mom's house. We have a dog. We have a pool. We have friends. We have a life. All of these things she's been telling me these past few days feel like a story about someone else's life. My presence — my role — in any of it, even here in the hospital, feels unreal. Fake. I feel like a stand-in. It's as if my entire life is a play and everyone in it are actors, pretending. For a moment, I think I might actually remember a movie like that, but that memory is gone too. I know I'm over-thinking things again. The doctor tells us that I should approach things one day at a time and just take it as it comes. I hope against hope that I remember, but I promise myself that I won't let the fear take over again, regardless. Everything seems to be happening so fast and I can't keep it all straight in my head.

The nurse, as if in response to my scattered thoughts, walks in pushing an empty wheelchair.

"Ready to rock and roll, Steve-O?"

I've never been less ready for anything in my entire life — well, in the life that I can recall, that is.

"I was born ready." I lie.

3

It's almost dark when we leave the hospital. The surroundings aren't familiar to me and I wonder if that's because it's too dark, or if along with my past, geographical markers have also escaped my conscious. Lisa went ahead to get the car, and she pulls up to the hospital entrance a few minutes later. It's not a car. It's a big, black pick-up truck. The nurse helps me into the truck and after a few exchanged pleasantries and goodbyes, we drive off. The formality of our parting masking my mounting anxiety. Cutting directly across the street into a pharmacy drive-thru, Lisa hands the pharmacist my information. The doctor called ahead for mild pain relievers. That's it. No sedatives. Nothing too strong. While we wait, Lisa reaches over and gently grabs my hand.

"I didn't suspect you'd be driving a big redneck truck,"I jest, trying to ease the tension. I'm at a loss for any real chit-chat.

"Haha," she says dryly. "This is your truck, pal. My car is in the shop. So I guess that means you're the redneck?"

She laughs. I laugh back. Neither one of them real laughter, but we've passed the time and granted the awkwardness a reprieve. Lisa gets the meds and we head out onto the main road. I scan the scenery for any sign of recognition but it's just too dark to really see anything clearly. Surprisingly, I see a few things I recognize. Some of these places I can recall perfectly. The Cajun restaurant with its mismatched window blinds. I remember how good their spicy rice is. The tire store. I remember the giant pothole at the entrance to it. A gas station, the high school, the used bookstore. I recognize all of these places, yet they've changed from how I remember them. They look old. Black, white, and grey, as if they've been replaced by an aged newspaper print of their former selves. I grew up in this town, I remember that too. But this is like coming back home after having moved away for a long, long time. It gives me an uneasy feeling, as if I've been in a coma for years instead of a few days. Lisa tells me that we had our house built roughly six years ago, yet the aged buildings I see look ancient. Tired of straining my eyes to see, I lie back and close them, lost in thought for what seems like only a few minutes. I feel the wheels slow down as we pull off of the road. Opening my eyes, I see it's a neighborhood. I recognize the entry gate. As she goes to punch in the code, I remember it.

"1682!" I call out. Then I recall that we picked this code because it's the name of a Chinese restaurant that we used to order from back in college.

"The restaurant!" I shout.

"Yes!" she says. Her eyes mist up a little — out of excitement or uneasiness, I'm not sure — but no more tears for now. I high-five her, but I don't tell her the truth. I remember the restaurant. I think I remember going there with her. But in my memory, her face and her voice are missing. She's like a blank space. A write-your-name-here space.

"Anything else coming to you?" she asks.

"Not much else really," I tell her. I realize that I'm starting to feel guilty every time I have to admit that I can't remember things, as if I've somehow chosen this over the memory of her. We pull past the gate and I look at the houses along the street. I don't recognize any of this, and the optimism I'd gained from the gate code and the restaurant starts to slip away just as fast as the memories came back.

Lisa had her mom keep Tyler for one more night, to give me a chance to get acclimated to being at home. She takes a right then a left turn through the neighborhood and I keep wondering if each house coming up is ours. Finally, we pull into the driveway of a two-story beige and brown stucco house. It has a two-car garage and the front yard looks recently mowed. A portable basketball net stands on a pole on the side of the driveway. The house looks nice, but the familiarity of it is just out of reach. We both get out of the truck at the same time. Part of me can't wait to get inside, to see what, if anything, might trigger my memory. But I'm also afraid to set foot in the house. What if nothing looks familiar? What is nothing opens the floodgates of days gone by? What if I never get my memory back? The thought of spending the rest of my life like this makes a little hot spot in the pit of my stomach. Lisa grabs a box from the car with the few remaining flowers and vases in it from the hospital. I wonder who those are from. I feel a sudden urge to look through them, to see if they spark a memory. I remember the doc's advice and force myself to wait. I grab the backpack of my old clothes and the bag from the pharmacy and follow her to the front door.

Lisa fumbles her key into the lock with one hand, balancing the box in the other. Pushing the door open with her foot, a squat little brown and white bull dog immediately pokes his head through, like he was just waiting for the door to open.

"Hi, Annie!" she says.

The dog starts wiggling like crazy. Ah, a girl dog, I mentally correct myself. "Hi, Annie," I say.

She comes wiggling over and licks the leg of my jeans. I

reach down and pat her on the head with my good hand. She's certainly happy to see me. We push past into the entry way and I take in the room. The house is open and airy. I can see the dining room, living room, and kitchen from the front foyer. There's a pile of newspapers on the kitchen counter, likely stacked there from her mom dropping by over the past week. The furniture and decorations look earthy. Lots of brown and beige. I like it. It's sort of minimalistic, but classy. A couple of abstract paintings hang in the living room. Clay pots align the fireplace mantle. Everything looks very clean and organized. It certainly doesn't look like the house that a four-year-old lives in. Either Lisa is constantly cleaning, or we have a maid. Following her into the kitchen, I set everything down on the counter next to the newspapers. She takes my hand.

"I'm not going to keep asking if you remember. I know you'll tell me when you do." She half-smiles for just a brief moment.

I notice that she'd said *when* and not *if.* She's staying positive, and that too is a comfort.

"Come, let me give you the grand tour of your own house." She laughs a little, and again I note how strong she is. I laugh a little too, even though I'm terrified. I can see why I am attracted to her, yet I can't pretend that I actually remember her. She walks me through the living room.

"This is actually the only room we debated when we had the house built," she says. "I felt like it was cozy, but you said it was way too small."

Then it hits me.

"I remember! You said we could be that much closer, and I joked that I needed my space." She grins, but she doesn't ask me if there's anything else coming back. There isn't, and the grace in which she is starting to accept my little flashes of memories saves me from having to tell her that. It makes me feel a ping of something for her. Love? As we walk from room to room, nothing else comes back. I feel a vague sense of familiarity with the layout of the house, but nothing specific. Recalling these little things with Lisa, yet not actually remembering her scares me all over again. What if I get all of my memories back except real memories of her? What if she is forever this little blank placeholder in my mind, a persona without a physical identity? When we get to the bedrooms, I feel myself involuntarily squeezing her hand. The doors are shut and as we approach the first door in the hallway, I see a little homemade sign hanging on it that says, 'No Girls Uhlowd!'

"Well, looks like you'll have to wait here." I smile.

"Oh no, he specifically told me that this doesn't apply to mommies," she informs me. Technically, Lisa and the dog are the only girls in the house. So, the sign really makes no sense then, which makes it that much cuter. She opens the door and I immediately see that Tyler has a plastic bottle cap collection. The kind you see on milk jugs. He has them in plastic screw-top jars, color sorted, all along a low hanging shelf. There are hundreds of them.

"Wow, we must drink a lot of milk," I comment.

Lisa gives me a strange look. "What do you mean?"

"I just meant...It doesn't matter. His room is nice," I say.

I briefly wonder if the bottle caps are a strange thing for a kid to collect. The rest of the room is sparsely decorated, like the rest of the house. A small bed with green pine tree patterned blankets. There's a dresser with a small television sitting on it, a wooden toy chest and a large plastic bin with compartments of carefully sorted matchbox cars in the corner. Looking around the room, I fight back the sadness that I feel coming on. I don't even know my own son. I've never really been much of a kid person, and I now realize that I am actually remembering this about myself. This makes me feel an even greater wave of sadness. A boy whose father can't remember him, but doesn't like kids anyway. Suddenly, I feel like I can't catch my breath. A soreness in my body, my head. A sharp pain in my broken finger springs to life. I have to get out of this room. I half run back to the hall with Lisa following close behind.

"Hey... It's okay. It's okay, honey. Just take it slowly. Maybe giving you the tour was too much, too fast." She is single-hand-edly holding her life and mine together at the same time, yet she's almost apologetic.

"I'm fine," I lie. "What could I do? Somehow avoid parts of the house? No, I needed this. I'm fine." Again, a lie. I don't know what I need. In order to know that, I'd need to know who I am and what I want. And right now what I want is clarity, yet I'm trying to force some type of familiarity out of this situation that isn't presenting itself.

The only room left is our bedroom, and I'm terrified to go in there, more so than I was to even walk into this house. I don't know why. Am I afraid of more intimate reminders of a life I can't remember? I feel like my knees are shaking. I'm trying to hide it, but she must detect my feelings.

"Fair enough. But even so, we're taking a break from the tours" she says, then leads me back to the kitchen and over to one of the bar stools.

"Sit," she says.

I take a seat, and she pulls a bottle of wine from a small wicker wine rack on the kitchen counter. I take a deep breath, trying to center myself and calm down a little. Turning in my seat, I look out through the sliding glass back doors.

"We do have a pool," I state the obvious.

"Yes, a pool we never use," a hint of playful sarcasm in her voice, as if this has been a complaint. Of mine or of hers, I'm not sure.

She hands me a glass of red wine. I take a sip. It's strong. I take a couple of big gulps.

"Easy, babe. We aren't sure what caused your fall yet. Don't go all booze hound on me." She winks.

The wine starts working almost immediately, and I feel better. I close my eyes and focus solely on myself for a moment. I know who I am. I know my own personality. My likes and dislikes...and that's something. A place to start. It could have been worse, I tell myself. I could have forgotten who I am. I down the rest of my wine and hold up my empty glass. She pours me another.

"This is it for you, though. At least for now," she says.

I walk over to the counter where we came in and rummage through the pharmacy bag with my working hand. Pulling out my pain pills, I realize that I can't get the cap off with one hand.

"Can you give me a little help here?" I ask.

She opens the bottle and pours out two small white pills.

"Maybe you should try to eat a little something before you take these?" she suggests.

I know she's right. The steak was hours ago, but I don't feel like eating. I want to sleep. I want to sleep and wake up with my full memory back. Maybe that'll happen. I mean, it is possible seeing as I'm now in a place that is my home with my things surrounded by visual prompts of my life...our life, as a family. I pop the pills in my mouth and wash them down with the rest of my wine.

"I'm okay," I express. She seems a little relieved.

"I think I'd like to lie down. Maybe see if I can sleep." A yawn escapes my mouth in mid-sentence.

"Well, I'd like to sleep with you, Mr. Lewis." She's flirting with me, but I don't know her, and her calling me Mr. Lewis reminds me of the nurse, which reminds me of the hospital.

"No offense, babe, but you've got to get a shower," she says, pulling a black garbage bag from the cabinet under the sink. "Let's make sure and keep your cast dry."

Taking my hand again, she leads me back toward our bedroom. The wine is with me now, it's made a pleasant and peaceful place in the recesses of my mind, and I'm not as scared to go in there. She opens the door and I see inside our room. This room, like the house, is nicely decorated and well kept. Except the bed. It's a mess. Pillows on the floor. Blankets spread everywhere.

"We had fun in here right before you went to the kitchen for water...and...and you fell." Her voice fades then comes back. "I haven't made time to clean things up much since." She shuts the door behind her.

The room goes dark. The furniture is black. Black shades are pulled shut. Without the light coming in from the open door, it's hard to see in here. She flicks on a light in the attached bathroom and I continue to look around. The room is more crowded than Tyler's. A large dresser runs along the wall. A television perched on a separate high dresser. A king-sized bed with matching night stands. A shiny silver lamp on the right one, an alarm clock beside it. Next to them, a copy of a movie magazine with an actor's face I don't recognize. On the wall, a framed oil painting of a bright red mailbox. It's a whimsical and playful piece of art. It looks like it belongs in a kids' room. It's out of place in here. Everything in here is somewhat familiar to me, except the mailbox painting.

I follow her into the bathroom. She puts the trash bag on the counter, and pulls her white t-shirt off. My fear is dissolving fast, and I am immediately lost in her body. Her smooth, freckled, pale skin. She one-handedly snaps off her bra, then turns away from me to take off her pants. I'm a little embarrassed by my sudden urge to see her naked. She pulls down her jeans with her panties still in them, then spins toward me. Now I see her full bare breasts, right in my face.

"Arms up," she orders.

I'm completely distracted, but I comply and lift my arm. awe of this woman who knows I don't remember her yet strips down in front of me like it's the most mundane thing she's done today. She carefully pulls my shirt off over my arms, being careful not to bump my hand or rub my head with it.

"You HAVE to keep the bandage on your head until we see the doctor again next week, so try not to get it wet," she instructs me.

I don't remember the doctor saying that, but I wasn't really paying attention to his directions. She bends down and takes off my belt, unzips my pants and starts pulling them down. I'm trying to prevent it, but my manhood is rising. I feel like a high school kid trying not to get turned on by the hot, sexy teacher. By the time she slides my pants off my ankles, I'm fully aroused. As she starts pulling my boxer shorts down, she notices.

"Oh...maybe you do remember me?" she says, and I can't tell if she's being playful or serious, but right now, it doesn't matter.

She pulls me toward her, then turns her body away from me. Resting her hands on the edge of the bathtub, she peers over her shoulder back at me, her hair falling forward exposing her neck and her arched spine. Pushing back against me, she rubs herself on me. Suddenly, all I can think of is taking her. I push forward, gently sliding inside this foreign body. I silently condemn myself for fucking this stranger, but she knows me. She knows what I like, and I'm stripped down to more than just my nakedness now. I'm physically stripped of everything and anything I've ever known except this. This joining of two bodies, performing the most basic element of life, a consummation of two beings seeking a release. She's warm and wet. Soft, small moans fill the bathroom as she pushes harder against me. Her body is smacking against mine and I forget about the pain in my hand. I forget about my lost memories. I feel safe, I feel comfort, I feel joy. I feel pleasure. I can't stop myself. I can't slow down, and I'm quickly approaching a climax with her...then I smell that same perfume again. The jasmine. It stops me dead in my tracks. I know that perfume. It's not Lisa's. In this moment, this exact moment, I know that I am in love. I am madly in love...with someone else.

In this moment, I know that I have to remember.

4

I feign pain in my hand to end this.

"I'm sorry. I have stop. My hand is killing me."

"It's okay. I understand." She pulls away from me, attempting to straighten herself without it being obvious she's disappointed, she bends picking up the garbage bag. Gently, she wraps my broken hand with it, snapping the open end tight against my arm with a hair tie. We take a shower together without saying much. I feel like it's written all over my face, but it must not be. She seems like she's recovering from the awkward moment...happy now. Guilt wells up inside me again and I wonder if I really have been cheating on her. I must have. I know what I felt, in that moment, and echoes of that feeling are swarming around in my head. Maybe I'm just confused. Maybe I have some extensive brain damage that could not be seen by the tests. I feel the pain killers doing their magic. The wine mixes in nicely and suddenly I can barely keep my eyes open. She shuts off the water, towels us both off, and walks me to the bed. I sit down hard. Foggy. Everything is so foggy. I can hear her talking but I can't focus enough to hear the words. She smiles.

"Get some sleep, babe," she suggests, and I do. I sleep.

. . .

WAKING to the sound of her mumbling, I look over at the clock, it's 4:11 am. Lisa is facing away from me, wrapped up tight in the blankets. She is shivering.

"Are you okay?" I ask.

She doesn't respond and I notice that she's twitching now, shaking the bed.

"Lisa. Wake up. You're having a bad dream." I nudge her gently.

She stops twitching, then starts mumbling again..

"Promising... promising...promising," she mutters under her breath.

I nudge her again.

"Hey. It's okay. Wake up."

She keeps mumbling. "Promising."

Then I hear them, footsteps in the hall. Several sets of footsteps followed by low voices. A chill falls over me and all the hairs on the back of my neck stand up.

"Lisa!" I whisper as loud as I can. "Someone is in the house!"

She says it as clear as day this time. "Promising."

I start to get out of the bed when she immediately sits up, still facing away from me, toward the bathroom. I reach across to touch her when she whips her head around and...it's not her face. It's old. Mummified. Wrinkled. Leathery. Her eyes are still closed, and when she suddenly opens them wide, one is blue and the other green. She smiles a terrifying smile of old, crooked, yellow teeth and says it as clear as day this time. "It's not looking promising."

I try to scream but nothing comes out.

5

I wake with a start. Covered in sweat. Still in bed. I hear Lisa's soft snoring. Looking over at the clock, again, it's 4:11 am. I listen for any noise. Then, I hear it again. Footsteps in the hall. Different this time. Lighter, and moving at a faster pace, yet coming closer and closer. A cold panic starts taking over. The footsteps stop right outside of the bedroom door. I notice Lisa didn't close it completely and as I strain to see through the thin crack of the opening, the door starts to slowly open. My heart is pounding when the door stops. It's only about a foot open but no one is there. Then I look down. Annie comes trotting in. I lie back in bed for minute, my heart still beating out of my chest.

"You scared the shit out of me dog," I say.

She must need taken out. I'm not getting any more sleep tonight anyway. Still shaking from the dream and the door, I get out of bed and move to the closet. Rummaging through the clothes, I can only find a robe that must be Lisa's. It's white, with a Mercedes emblem on it. I think she's slightly obsessed with Mercedes. I put on the robe. It's a little too tight, and I probably look ridiculous. I head down the hall, Annie following behind.

"Okay, girl, where's your leash?" I ask her, as if she'll answer.

Looking through the coat closet near the back door. No luck. Just a bunch of books and a few photo albums. I decide to chance it and take her out without a leash. She follows me out the back door, then takes off running towards the back of the yard. Great. I've lost the dog. Walking in the direction she went, I find her behind a stack of freshly trimmed limbs, doing her business.

"Sorry, girl. I thought you left me." She tilts her head, giving me a curious look.

When we get back inside, I decide to leaf through the photo albums I'd stumbled upon in the coat closet. I tell myself that I'm not going to over analyze them. Just flip through them, casually. The first album is white with the words "Life Is Not Counted In Days, But In Memories" printed on it. I wonder what that makes my life now. Opening the book, the first few pictures are of various places. A beach. A sunset. An old grey picnic table, it's paint worn and chipping off, and a field of blue flowers in the background. Flipping a few more pages, a windmill, a church with an ornate stained glass window depicting a sunrise. Why would we have a photo album full of pictures with no people? I wonder. Maybe one of us is an amateur photographer or something. Setting the book on the couch, I walk over to grab the other album. It's made of red leather and bound with a thin brown rope. It looks ancient, like a spell book from a fantasy novel. I take it back to the couch and plop down a little too hard, sending a little jolt of pain up my side, down my arm and into my injured hand. Note to self, don't do that again.

Opening the cover, I see more pictures. The pages of the album yellowing, the pictures are old and faded. They look like they're from an old Polaroid instant-film camera. The kind where the pictures print right out of the camera. The first few images are of a little kid. Maybe a boy, around age five or so. In each shot, he's carrying a yellow popsicle and standing in someone's driveway. Nothing looks familiar so I turn the page. More pictures of the boy. He has curly brown hair and he's not wearing a shirt. He's only a wearing a diaper and brown cowboy boots. Scanning through more pictures, I see my dad standing in the background in some of the shots. A young version of him. I'm reminded of his absence.

I was only nineteen when he died. Strangely, I never really felt that horrible sadness one might expect when losing a parent. He was a good dad. The best, and even though he left us well before we would have expected, he lived a full life. A good life. I will always miss him, and that's comforting to me right now because I do remember him. The boy in these pictures must be me. Then it comes to me. I do remember this day. I got a haircut, right there in the driveway. We lived next to a hairdresser, and she'd cut the neighborhood families' hair for a discount. The popsicle was my prize for not being difficult about it. My father appeared in a few more pictures on the next page. He looks sad, depressed. In the last picture from this set, he's looking right at the camera, an expression of grief on his face. I don't recall ever seeing him look like this. It's so out of character that I'm lost in that for a moment. I wonder what was happening that day that had bothered him so. This isn't helping me. Flipping a few more pages, I see more pictures of myself as a kid. A birthday party. A bunch of kids wearing pointed party hats. I don't recognize anyone in the pictures. Nothing is familiar to me, except the house. It's my parents' house. The one I grew up in. I do remember that, and that's a good sign. I put the album aside and get up to grab the last one. The sun is coming up, marking the start of a new day. Another day without my memories. I shake off the thought and look back to the photos. The last album looks to be the newest. The cover is yellow plastic, with a little inset plastic frame on the cover. Looks like we never got around to putting a picture in it. I open it up to a picture of me and Annie in the pool. I'm floating on a green raft with her lying in my lap. She looks like she's sleeping. I look away from the book to the current-day Annie, lying in the middle of the floor. She sees me looking and walks over to lick my leg.

"Good dog." Giving her a quick pat on the head, I look back at the photos. More pictures of me in the pool. A few of me grilling burgers. There's a whole page full of pictures of Annie out in the backyard, running and rolling around. In another picture, my mom is sitting out in the sun, holding up a blue tinted glass of iced tea with a lemon wedge stuck to the side of it. I flip past a few more pages. Here's a picture of Lisa with Tyler sitting in her lap. It looks like this picture was taken in a studio. Something is off with this picture. Something's not quite right and, at first glance, I can't put my finger on it..

"What are you doing?!" Her voice scares me so bad that I drop the album.

"Whoa! Why the yelling?" I ask.

Lisa is standing at the end of the hall, wearing an oversized Mercedes t-shirt and zebra striped pajama bottoms. She is visibly frazzled.

"I just meant...you're supposed to be taking it slow." She seems to be trying to compose herself. "Then I find you here at the crack of dawn, going through pictures."

She walks over and gently picks the album up off the floor. Snapping it shut, she eyes me in an odd way. "I'm just worried about you. That's all. Sorry if I scared you."

Stacking the albums back in the closet, she turns to me.

"Ready for breakfast?"

6

After a quick and relatively silent breakfast of plain toast and coffee, Lisa tells me that she has to take Annie to the vet today, and then run by our office to check on things. She's been managing things since my accident. Her comments make it apparent that we've got a very supportive staff. She's only had to drop in here and there to sign checks and such.

"It's been pretty easy, really," she says. "I've been going by a few times a week just to make sure everything is running smoothly. I'll keep doing that for a while, at least until you feel good enough to get back to it."

I can't imagine going there. I know nothing about running a company, much less about the painting business. Is this really my life now? Why does the thought of me owning a paint company cause me to inwardly die of boredom?

"It's going to be a little busy for me today," she mentions. "The vet to drop off Annie, the office, the vet again to pick her up, then over to my mom's to get Tyler. Whew."

"I wish I could help," I throw out there, although I know I it isn't even possible as I have no idea who these people are much less where these places are located. "I guess I'm going to just hang around here today."

"That WILL help." She smiles. "You need to rest to get better, and we need you to get better. So here you'll stay until you're all rested up."

Her last statement comes off as more of an order. It makes me a little uncomfortable, but I agree. Maybe if I explicitly follow the doctor's orders, my full memory will come back. I hit the couch and fumble with the remote, trying to figure out how to get something on the TV. She's dressed and heading out the door by the time I find something to watch.

"I shouldn't be gone too long," she says, fumbling to get a leash on Annie.

Then, as if she just recalled that I can't remember anything, she adds, "The office is only a couple of miles from here, and mom's a couple more from there. The vet is kind of in between the two. So, unless the office is a disaster, I should only be gone for a few hours." She pauses.

"I'll call you when I'm heading home. Okay? Maybe I'll pick up pizza for dinner," she yells from the door, and just like that, I'm alone.

She's long gone by the time I realize that I don't even know where the phone is. I guess I'll find it when she calls. Finally getting the TV working, I flip through the channels. I don't recognize anything. How could I have forgotten so much? How could the doctor not see anything wrong with my brain? Lisa placed a call to Dr. Lambert this morning, confirming my appointment for Monday. He's a specialist with these types of scenarios. Knowing that gives me a spark of hope. That only leaves the weekend between now and then, but it seems like an ocean of time. Two more days of not knowing what's wrong, and perhaps even worse, wondering if they'll ever find out what's really happening to me. How can they fix what they can't diagnose? I stop the channels on a rerun of *Andy Griffith*. I recognize this. I used to watch it when I was a kid, and I again find comfort in little memories. Stretching out on the couch, I feel my body relaxing. This is how I'll be able remember things, by relaxing. Watching for what only seems like a few minutes, I suddenly wake from a nap. I had dozed off. *The Beverly Hillbillies* are on now. I know this one too. The phone is ringing. Lisa calling, I'm sure. I shake off the nap and make for the kitchen. The ringing is coming from in there. I see the cordless phone on the wall and pick up the receiver.

"Hello?" I wait. Then I hear my mom's voice.

"Hi, honey. It's your mother." She speaks as if she thinks I might not remember her either. I'm speechless for a moment.

"I'm so sorry," she says.

Still trying to find my voice, I say, "No, no, I'm glad you called. It's nice to hear a voice I recognize. How are you?"

I try to sound lighthearted. I'm not sure if it's working.

"Oh, Stephen, I've been so worried. I am so worried." Then, after a little pause, she asks, "Can he even hear me?" She's speaking to someone else in her room.

Indeed, she does sound tired.

"I hear you, Mom. I'm okay. I'm remembering a lot. I just... I'm sure she's told you, but—I don't remember Lisa. I don't remember Tyler either. I'm trying to keep it together but—it's challenging."

She doesn't say anything for so long, I start to think the phone lost connection.

Finally, I her her say, "Well...it's in God's hands now. The best we can all do is pray."

My mom knows that I'm not much for religion. It's been a point of contention between us for many years. I'm wondering if this is her way of seeing if I remember that, and maybe hoping that I don't. She continues.

"I would have come to see you, but you know, my hip."

It comes to me then, a memory. My mom's broken hip. Her long road of physical rehabilitation. Her never being quite able to get around very easily ever since. Her moving into an assisted living facility.

"I know, Mom. I know. I'm sure all of my memories will come back. The doctor says it'll just take some time. Anyway, how are you?"

My attempt to change the subject doesn't work.

"I hope you come out of this soon, Stephen. I pray you do," she replies.

"Well, things are coming to me slowly. I still don't remember anything about that night. I can barely even remember this house. I have to just take it slow, or it gets really scary. It gets scary anyway, really, but I'm holding out okay," I add.

She's silent again for a moment, and it's here that I start to remember the relationship I have with my mom...or lack thereof. My dad and I were very close, and right now I wish I could talk to him. He'd have some joke about the situation and it wouldn't be funny, but it would make us both feel better anyway. She's still not saying anything, so I do.

"Mom, I need to go. I need to get some rest. Thanks for calling. I'll keep you posted on things."

After yet another moment of silence, she replies, "Take care of yourself, Stephen. You'll be in my prayers."

We end the call, and I stand in the kitchen for a moment. Feeling a little agitated at my mom, for reasons I can't quite pinpoint. Maybe her incessant belief that simply uttering her prayers will be the cure for my memory loss. But it's more than that. It's my childhood with her. It's the way she always treated my father, like he wasn't quite good enough for her. Not godly enough. Realizing that I still have the phone in my hand, I hang it back on the wall. Heading back to the couch, I hear it. At first I think it might be the TV show. I sit back down on the couch and listen for it. Nothing. It was my head. Just as I stretch out on the couch, I hear it again. Searching the couch for the remote, I hear it yet a third time. Footsteps in the hall. This time it's not Annie. She's gone to the vet. This time, I know I'm not dreaming.

Finally finding the remote, I shut the TV off and listen. It sounds like someone walking by the opening of the hallway every few minutes. In between, I hear chatter. People talking in low voices. Distant. Then, a chime. The sounds aren't as distant this time. I can hear them clearly. Slowly, I sit up. The leather on the couch creaking loudly. Standing, as quietly as I can, I tiptoe over to the entryway between the hall and the front door. I still hear it. Listening intently now, I hear one set of footsteps quicken a bit and then get louder. They are coming right toward me. I'm tempted to dart off but I wait and watch. I can't see anything from this angle, yet they get louder and louder. I can't stand the anticipation. I step out into the hall and chance looking. A bright light shines directly in my right eye, completely blinding. The vision in my other eye goes pitch black.

I cry out. "Hey!"

A voice responds, "You can hear me?!"

Then, I can see again. The light is gone. The footsteps and the voices are gone. Nothing. Silence. The hallway empty and dimly lit from the kitchen light. I can hear the faint sound of a bird outside and a car driving by. I wait. Listen. Nothing else but the bird and then another car. For a second, I reflect on how both the bird and the driver of the car know where they are going, so unlike me. I slink down the wall and sit on the floor. Looking down the hall I still see nothing. My only company a painting of palm trees hanging on the wall.

What is happening to me? I feel like I'm losing my mind. Getting back up, I walk up and down the hall for the next twenty minutes or so. Looking. Listening. Nothing abnormal. Making my way around the house. I check the front door, the side door, the door to the garage, the back door. All locked. I walk back to the couch and sit. My head is hurting again. I feel exhausted. Was I hallucinating? Maybe I just need more sleep. I know that I'm trying to rationalize things. Back in the kitchen, I struggle to get the top off of the bottle of the pain pills. It's no use. I can't get the lid off with one hand. I should have had Lisa put them in something easier to open. Pressing the edge of the bottle on the ledge of the counter, I apply pressure.

Here, now, I'm starting to feel like I'm truly falling apart. I feel my knees start to buckle just as the lid pops off. Standing back up, I swallow two pills down dry and go back to the couch. I'm afraid to sleep. I'm afraid to stay awake. Sleep takes me sooner than I expected, and with it, an unexpected gift.

The sun is in my face, but it feels nice.

We're driving with the top down. Her hair is flying around in the wind. The day is gorgeous. She is gorgeous. I couldn't be any happier than I am with her right here, right now. If ever there were such a thing as love, this is it.

"Looks like a mellow weekend coming up, for a change," I say. She smiles that crooked little smile I know so well. She's beautiful, and I'm lost in that for a moment before she replies.

The beep of a car alarm arming wakes me. I feel tears on my face. Listening, I hear Lisa talking outside...and Tyler. They are home. The doorknob is rattling. Wiping my face, I sit up and try to put on a happy face. The door bursts open and in runs a little kid. Full speed, right into my lap.

"Tyler, be careful, honey. Daddy's still sore from his fall," Lisa tells him, walking in behind, carrying a large pizza box with "Rory's" printed on the side. I know that place. I remember it. Annie comes trotting in between her feet.

"Hi, Daddy! Look what I got!" Tyler pulls a Matchbox car out of his pocket. It's a cement mixer truck.

"I didn't have this one yet!" he exclaims.

"Wow! That's great!" I reply, a bit overenthusiastically.

He acts like nothing has happened. Like it's just another day with mom and dad. I don't recognize anything about him. Maybe his face, a little. Maybe. I don't recognize my own family. Hell, I'm seeing things that aren't really there. I push down the urge to fall apart again.

"Momma said we can watch a movie after dinner! My choice!" He's so excited to see me.

More guilt. I feel like I've emotionally abandoned him. I feel no connection to him, or to her for that matter. But I also feel angry. Angry at the person I must have been to have strayed when I had this loving family. I know it's true. There is someone else. I'm sure of it. My emotions are at war with each other, a battle that can't have a clear winner. This other woman, whoever she is...I feel a growing urge to find out who she is. I feel a deep longing for her. Yet I feel a sense of obligation to my family. What have I done? Did I do this to myself? The fall. Was it on purpose? An act of self loathing for the harm I was ultimately causing my family?

Tyler interprets my silence as disinterest in watching a movie with him. "We don't have to," he mumbles, a little disappointed. "You can pick this time."

He perks back up at the thought of me choosing the movie.

"SpongeBob, it is!" I say, for lack of any idea of what he likes, or what kids' movies even exist, for that matter. I feign enthusiasm with my response.

"Awesome!" he shouts, and then bursts off to his room, eager to add the new Matchbox car to his collection.

I'm realizing now that I'm going to have to play along, at least until I remember, if I ever remember. If I don't, then I suppose I'll have to play along forever. The thought of that sounds like a living hell, and I force myself to stop focusing on it. I'll remember. Day by day. I will. But the visions, the dreams, the footsteps. Will they go away as I remember things?

Lisa has the pizza box open and I smell it. I remember. I've been to Rory's pizza many times. I love their pizza. I always get the garlic lover's (a specialty of theirs), but I add mushrooms, extra cheese, and extra garlic. But I have never been there with Lisa. Of this, I am suddenly certain, and it starts to come back to me now. This pizza place was off the beaten path. It's not anywhere near Lisa's mom's house, the vet, or the office. I accidentally found it when I was out for a drive in the country. The initial charm of it was the remote location. It sits beside an ancient gas station way out on Route 16. I remember now. A little red brick building with an old maroon canopy above the entrance. Bright green vines climb the walls around the dusty windows. Splotches of multi-colored potted flowers sit below the building's windowsills, probably fake. The sign by the road is so old that it's hard to read. I've been there many times, but never alone. This was our place. Not mine and Lisa's, but the other woman. We loved this place. The food. The atmosphere. Each other's company. The fact that no one we know would see us together way out there was the initial draw. The only way Lisa would have gone there would have been on purpose, and if she did that, then she knows about her. Is she messing with me? Some sort of revenge for cheating on her?

"Come get it while it's still warm!" she yells from the kitchen.

I can't play the part here until I know what's going on. I walk towards the kitchen.

"I think I know this pizza place," I say. "Isn't it kind of far away?"

"You remember!" She smiles and winks at me.

"Yes, it is a little far. But it's your favorite pizza, so it was worth the drive. It's only barely warm though, so eat up. Garlic lover's with mushrooms, extra cheese and extra garlic. Just the way you like it." She winks again.

I play dumb, trying to hide the shock I'm feeling. Am I remembering this incorrectly? No, I'm not. I'm sure of it.

I play along. "Sounds like a weird combo, but you were right about that steak in the hospital, so I'm in." I try to wiggle out a slice with one hand.

"I can't remember how I know that place."

She replies. "We were out driving one day and just came

across it. Remember, they have that smelly old guy in there who plays the accordion?"

I do remember. He's just an old hired musician but we secretly called him Rory. We. The other woman and me. Not Lisa. She's pretending that this was us together, but it wasn't. She is testing me to see what I remember. Is she hoping to replace my memories of this woman with her instead? A strong sense of anger comes over me. Whatever emotional pain that I have caused my wife, it does not warrant her playing with my memories like this.

"I don't remember going there with you," I say, point blank.

"Well, you don't even remember me at all, so I wouldn't expect that you would," she says, her voice going flat.

Is she upset that I didn't fall for her little trick?

"The accordion guy, I do remember him. His name was..." I wait.

She jumps in, "Rory! Hahaha!" and she laughs on for a moment, as if we share some funny memory of that.

"Yes. Rory!" I fake a chuckle.

"You're coming around, babe. Little by little, it will all come back. I just know it," she says.

But what has me worried more than her trying to manipulate my memories is how she would know this. I don't remember how many times I've been to the pizza place, but I know I went there many times with this other woman. This means Lisa must have followed us there. That would explain how she knew about this place. But how would she know what I ordered? Could she have obtained a copy of the receipt from them? That theory seems thin. How would she know that we called the musician Rory? I remember that this was an inside joke. We never even really said it out loud while in the restaurant. If she knows a little private detail like this, then she has spoken to the other woman. I have to find out who the other woman is.

Two hours and one pain pill later, we're sitting on the couch watching a SpongeBob movie. It's awful, which is just as well. Tyler is asleep beside me. His hand still resting on a half-eaten bowl of popcorn. Lisa is on the other side of me, thumbing through a magazine.

"Hey, has the house ever been robbed?" I ask.

"What?" she replies. I turn the TV down a little bit.

"Have we ever been robbed?" I ask again.

"I heard you, I was just surprised at the question. No. Why?" she asks, seemingly a little agitated.

"I just wondered," I start, suddenly not sure if I want to tell her about the footsteps or the flashlight that I've seen from the apparently invisible robbers.

I decide to tell her anyway. "I had a bad dream about us being robbed today during my nap."

She sits upright. "Exactly what happened in your dream?" she asks, suddenly overly interested.

"I thought I heard footsteps. Maybe saw a flashlight...or something," I reply, unsure of how much to tell her.

"You thought you heard footsteps coming down the hall? That's creepy, babe, but given what you've been through, I'm not surprised you had a scary dream." She dismisses my comments as if swatting away a fly.

But I never told her where I heard the footsteps in the house. I never said "the hallway." Suddenly a little voice in my head tells me not to trust her, and then I wonder if I should trust that little voice. Should I trust anything from my own head? Does Lisa have people spying on me when she's not around to make sure I don't leave? To make sure that I don't find the other woman again? But that wouldn't explain the "visitors" magical disappearing act.

"Yes, a lot of things have been scary lately," I reply.

9

Friday morning. I actually slept last night. I did take one more pain pill before bed. Not so much for physical pain, but to help with sleep. No dreams for once. No haunted hallway either. I figured out how to set the bedside alarm and did so for seven A.M. I also figured that I'd tell Lisa I wanted to go for an early morning walk. Get some fresh air. But she slept right through the alarm, so there's no need for that discussion. Feeling a little refreshed for a change. I decided I'm going to stay off the pills today to keep my head clear. Carefully, I crawl out of bed and creep around the room, throwing on the first clothes I can find. A grey sweatshirt and well-worn jeans. At least these clothes are mine. It takes me forever to get the shirt over my head with one hand and without waking her. I can't tie my shoes, so I improvise and tuck the laces down into them. Escaping the room unnoticed, I make my way out into the hall. I need to get out of this house and see what else triggers my memory. I can't help but feel like Lisa is hiding something. I feel like she is lying to me. I need to find out what she's lying about, and why. Halfway down the hall, I can hear Tyler in his room. It sounds like he's acting out a movie or something. As I pass his closed door, I hear Annie scratching from the inside of his room. She probably needs to go outside but I don't want to jeopardize my escape. I walk as quietly as I can past his door and head for the kitchen. I find paper and a pen in the first drawer I try. Did I remember where we keep those? Or was it the luck of the draw? I quickly scratch a note.

Went for a walk to get some fresh air. Won't be gone long. - Steve

As I'm heading for the door, I realize how silly it was for me to put my name. Just because I don't know my wife doesn't mean that she doesn't know me. The truth is, she probably knows me better than I do, and I'm starting to think maybe I'm not nearly as likable as she's making me out to be, or as she wants me to be. Heading out the front door, I cut across the driveway to the side patio to avoid getting all wet from the grass. There, leaning against the house, I see a bicycle. My bicycle. Perfect. I hop on and start peddling, suddenly aware of how ridiculous I probably look. Bandaged forehead, arm in a cast, riding a bike. But it doesn't matter. I don't care how I look. I'm free of the house. Free to go where I want to go. Free to explore the possibility that there are things I'm not being told, and that maybe I'm purposely being kept in the dark.

Heading straight for the neighborhood gate, I'm betting that I won't see many people this early in the morning. I'm right, although I do pass a few. An older lady getting her mail. A kid getting the newspaper from his driveway. A middle-aged man bringing his garbage can in from the road. None of them pay me any attention, so I'm assuming that they don't know me. Pedaling the bike with my injuries is more difficult than I thought, and I have to lean heavily on my good side. When I get to the front of the neighborhood, I realize my dilemma. The community gate at the end of the sidewalk requires a key to get in or out. The road has an automatic gate, but it's only triggered by the weight of a vehicle. Not a bike. No one is coming or going into the neighborhood now, so I'm locked in. Not that I had any real destination in mind. I decide to pass the gate and scope out the rest of the neighborhood instead. The road curves around to a series of houses that all look very similar to each other. In between some of these are empty lots that apparently never sold. They aren't developed and have grown thick with trees and brush. I pull off into a heavily wooded lot and stop the bike, climbing off and walking it through the underbrush. Maneuvering the bike through the brush and thick branches is a challenge with one hand, and turning to look back to the road, I realize just how wooded these lots are. I'm only thirty feet from the road but I can no longer see it. Pushing forward, the bike's tires tangle up in a vine and it takes me a few minutes to unwind it with one hand. Finally moving deeper into the lot, I break from the trees into a small clearing. There's an ornate block wall at the back of the lot, running the length of this side of the neighborhood. It's got a well-traveled path running alongside it. Walking the path, I see the neighborhood kids have been here. Random carvings and graffiti mark the wall in a few spots. A bright blue kite rests against the wall, tangled in string. An old knotted rope hangs over the wall a little further down the path. It's tied to some point on the other side. This wall is probably eight feet high. I continue walking along until I reach the edge of the woods. If I go any further in this direction, I'll be in someone's back yard. Turning around, I quicken my pace a bit. If I'm gone too long, Lisa will get worried. Or is it suspicious? In any case, I need to hurry. I retrace my steps back toward the road when I hear something rustling nearby in the brush. I quickly stop and listen. Perhaps it was an animal, but now I hear nothing. I'm starting to wonder about the nature of the noises I keep hearing and the light I saw in the hall. I'm the only one to witness these occurrences, and thus, I have to face the very real possibility that they could be purely in my head. I lean the bike against a tree and walk in the general direction of the noise. Cutting around a thicket of leaves and vines, I see a few small open sections of sandy soil. There are several footprints in them. The kind you'd expect to see from a man's dress shoe. They look fresh. Either I'm going crazy, becoming paranoid, or someone is definitely following me. I rush back to the bike and push on. When I get back to the road, I decide to head back to the house and give up on this adventure for now. I can probably cut through the neighborhood and get there sooner, but I'm unsure of the way, so I go back the way I came. Looking back behind me, I see no one. Keeping a steady pace back toward the front of the neighborhood, I see a little red sports car backing out of a driveway into the road. As the car turns toward the entrance, I speed up. I can follow them to the entry gate and get out!

Changing my mind again, I decide to leave the neighborhood. I start pedaling faster, pumping my legs and trying like hell to keep up. The car follows the curve of the road back around and slows to turn toward the gate. Perfect. Just as the gate starts to open, I make a quick glance back over my shoulder again to see if I'm being followed. Suddenly, I hit a small pile of pine needles and my front tire slips on the road. I over-correct and sling the bike off the pavement, stopping it dead in someone's front lawn, causing me to fly off the seat. I go down hard on the grass, raising my bad arm up so it doesn't hit the ground. The bike falls beside me. I immediately stand back up to survey the damage. My hip hurts a little where I fell, but nothing major. The bike looks okay too, and I jump back on. By the time I get close to the gate, it's shut tight again. Great. Abandoning any hope of escaping my neighborhood today, I head back. Just as I make the turn toward the house, a small SUV passes me heading for the gate. I turn around and follow, careful of where I'm steering. The truck approaches the gate as it opens, and I follow it out. Just like that. Free.

Now what? Looking around, I see the main road to my right heads into more heavily wooded areas. Probably more neighborhoods, or just more woods. To my left the road climbs a hill, and it's the direction Lisa and I came from yesterday. I'll go that way. I'm starting to think I should have planned this out better. I don't know what I expect to find by riding a bike around the town. Feeling a sense of discouragement, I crest the hill and see a small shopping center off to the right. I recall a brief look at it on the way back from the hospital. A convenience store, a home repair store, and several small shops in between. The ridiculousness of my plan becoming more apparent by the minute, I cut across the road and through the convenience store parking lot. Leaning the bike against a bench, I walk along the shopping center sidewalk, unsure of what to do next. As I approach the home repair store, I see several people coming and going. Early risers ready to work over the weekend. I'm so lost. I don't recognize this place. I don't recognize any of these people. I don't know what I am doing here. I need to go back home and map out some sort of real plan. I need to know who this other woman is and why she is haunting my distant memories.

I've walked all the way to the opposite end of the shopping center. As I decide to call it off again and head back, I see another building behind it. It looks like it might be the back of a grocery store. If so, then this is likely the grocery store we normally go to. Maybe seeing more familiar territory will trigger more memories. Something not guarded or filtered. Something without tricks or lies. The nearest side of the store is blocked by a loading bay with a locked gate around it. I'll have to get around to the other side to get to the entryway. There's an alley that runs down between the home repair shopping center and the grocery store. It looks like I can use that to get to the other side, so I head down the alley. I'm about half way to the other end of it when I consider whether or not I should have left the bike so far away. If someone takes it, I'll have to walk all the way back home from here. Just as I consider turning back to get it, a figure steps out into the far end of the alley in front of me. He's too far away for me to see his face, and the sun is rising at his back, leaving his face and features cast in shadow. He appears to be wearing a suit and some kind of hat. Maybe a derby or a beret. I can't tell from here.

"Where are you going?" he asks loudly, and his voice is so familiar that I'm instantly lost in a puzzle of thought, trying to figure out who he is.

"I..." I begin to reply. "I'm just going..."

Then he speaks again, his voice thick and deep. "You aren't going anywhere. You're sitting still, lying down. You need to take control. You need to get back on your feet."

I wait to see if he's going to say anything else. Does he know what's going on with me? Do I know this person? Is this who's been following me or is it just some crazy transient? I know that voice. Though vague, his statement feels eerily close to my current situation. He says nothing, and the silence gives me enough time to recompose. He startled me at first, but now I'm starting to get angry. Whether he is real or a figment of my damaged brain, it doesn't matter. I'm getting tired of being so lost.

"Who the hell are you?" I ask.

"You know who I am," he replies. "I am part of you and you are part of me. Calm down and you will remember. You need to remember, Steve."

I have no idea who he is, and right now, I don't have much tolerance for vague mysterious conversation.

"Okay, well, whoever you are. Have a nice day," I say, and turn around to go back the way I came, toward the entrance of the alley. Looking back over my shoulder, I notice he's gone. I'm going back to the bike. I really don't know where I was going anyway. I'm probably suffering some kind of psychotic episode at this very moment. I'm afraid, and all I want right now is out of this alley. I look forward, back to where I entered the alley, and he's standing there. The same position, and roughly the same distance from me. Now in the opposite direction. The sun shining in his face.

"I'm not here to scare you," he replies, sensing my sudden fear. "I'm hear to help you. You need to take your life back."

I'm freaking out, yet tiring of this game.

"Then really help me and stop with the riddles and bullshit mystery," I say.

He speaks a little louder, and this time I hear something else in his voice. Something I did not notice before. Vulnerability. He sounds fragile. Worn out.

"A curse is a crutch," he says, and then I see his face. I remember.

He never got mad when I used profanity. He just made me feel silly for it. That was his little catchphrase about it. A curse is a crutch indeed. My head starts spinning and I have to sit down. Maybe lie down. I hunch down on my knees, then all the way down on my back. I'm passing out.

The man in the alley. He's my dad.

10

"You can't sleep here."

I open my eyes to a blond-haired, pimply-faced teenager staring at me. Straining to get my bearings, the teenager hovers over me. He's wearing a green and red plaid apron with Gregor's Grocers sewn in across the front in bright yellow script and a logo of a little red knight riding a cow. The knight is holding a javelin, like he's jousting.

The teenager leans in closer, his hair is a mess, the smell of his clove cigarette right in my face.

"Dude, you can't sleep here," he says.

I wonder how long I've been out. Not long, based on the sun. It looks like it's still before midday.

"I wasn't sleeping. I passed out," I express, still getting my wits about me.

He smiles, flicking the ashes off of his cigarette with his thumb.

"Dude. That's still sleeping. You have a heat stroke or something? I mean, I don't even care that you're hanging out back here, bro, but the cops patrol this place a couple times a day. You can't sleep here."

"Yeah, you said that." My aggravation showing. "I was just leaving."

I stand up slowly, afraid I'll feel faint again. I don't, but I'm suddenly dying of thirst.

"What happened, man? You get in a fight?" The teenager is still talking when I'm too far away to hear what he's saying.

I must look a mess. Bandaged head. Arm in a sling. Passed out in an alley. It's no wonder he thinks I was in a fight.

Heading back to my bike, I wonder if it's still there. It takes a few minutes to get back. During this time I'm coming to the conclusion that I very likely have a serious level of brain damage from the fall in my kitchen. Hearing phantom footsteps and seeing lights is bad. Having full-blown conversations with my father's ghost is something else altogether. I'm going to have Lisa call the doctor as soon as I get back to the house. No, I'm going to call him myself.

The bike is still right where I left it. The ride back is uneventful, and there are a couple of cars driving in a line through the front gate of my neighborhood, so I don't have to worry about getting back in.

Pulling my bike up to the house, I see activity through the window. She's up. I imagine this conversation won't be pleasant. I get the feeling she would rather keep me in the house and away from the truth, whatever that may be. I walk back through the front door. Annie comes trotting out to greet me.

"Hey, guys," I say, trying to sound nonchalant.

"Daddy! Look, I made an airplane!" Tyler comes running at me with a mixed glob of Play-Doh in his hands. It looks nothing like an airplane.

"That's cool!" I tell him.

"It doesn't really fly, you have to pretend." He clarifies.

He's a cute kid, although it doesn't feel like he's mine. I skip past that thought before it sticks too deep again. Tyler runs back to the kitchen table, eager to make more airplane globs. Walking out to the living room, I see Lisa sitting on the floor, organizing coupons into little piles.

"Hey, babe!" she exclaims. "I was a little worried when I got your note, but I guess I need to let you breathe if you're going to get better."

Wow. That's not what I expected.

"Yeah, I had a nice time. This is a big neighborhood," I say. "It seems older than six years. Were there a lot of houses in here when we built this one?" I ask.

"Yes. Yes, there were," she says, and her answer seems awkward, like she doesn't want to talk about that.

"Cool." I reply. "How old is the neighborhood?"

"Not sure." She says quickly, keeping her eyes on her coupons. She says nothing to follow up to my question. I get the sense that she's lying again.

"Well, anyway, I just biked around the neighborhood. The fresh air was great." I start to feel like I'm coming off a little too animated. Like I'm overselling it.

"Biked?!" She almost yells. "Oh, babe, are you crazy? Do you know how dangerous that is for you right now? What if you crashed and hit your head again? Your arm? We still don't know why you fell." Then she notices the grassy smear on the hip of my pants where I fell off the bike.

"You crashed!"

I take a breath. "Nope. I just rubbed up against some vines and stuff walking through some of the wooded lots in here."

"You're walking through the woods with a bike, in your condition?" She sounds genuinely concerned. "I'd feel more comfortable if you stayed out in public where you can get help if you need it."

"Okay. Fair enough," I reply, just to end this conversation.

I decide to hold off on calling the doctor. I have a growing fear that telling the doctor that I'm hearing voices or seeing ghosts will land me in a facility of sorts. The kind of facility where they keep you heavily medicated. Maybe I'm being paranoid, but being all doped up surely won't help my condition or my memory. I've got to try and get things together on my own...for now. I make a little promise to myself. If it gets worse I'll call the doctor, even if I leave some of the details of my condition out.

Looking back down at Lisa, I say, "The ride felt good for me, but I could use a little rest. I think I'll get a quick shower and take a nap." I head up to the bedroom.

"Okay, I'll come check on you in a little while," she tells me.

I'm feeling like a mouse in maze. I haven't a clue of how to get closer to the truth about this woman, much less being able to understand why I'm seeing things. I try to take a quick shower but getting my clothes off and operating the shower takes a lot of effort with one hand. Somehow, I manage. Finally, I climb into bed and review the conversation with my dad, or his ghost, or my own imagination, or whatever it was. I can't remember his exact words now. Something like, "You're falling down on the job...or...you need to get your life back." Was it real? Did the kid from the grocery store see him? I should have asked him. I probably would have sounded even more crazy than I looked. Maybe I am crazy now. An old saying pops into my head, proving that my memory works on some level: *The thing about crazy people is they don't now they are crazy. That's what makes them crazy.*

I close my eyes and try again to think back to the last memory I have before waking up in the hospital. It's no use, I'm getting nothing. I take a few deep breaths, trying to relax. Thinking of my life like a timeline, I try to determine where things changed. Where did I stop remembering?

11

L ying here, trying to remember, I suddenly feel very tired. Tired of worrying and wondering. Tired of being scared. Tired of being awake, yet afraid to sleep. Trying to remember where my memory stopped working feels impossible. It's like hopping backwards over the empty spot in my life and landing on the last solid memory before it. I feel like I'm swimming in a sea of giant waves. Growing tired. Looking for a life raft that must be out there in the darkness somewhere. It must be.

Just as I decide to end this useless exercise and follow the doctor's orders of taking it slow, an image appears in my mind. A room. It's an office. In my mind, I see an office building. The seventh floor. I remember the ride inside the elevator and how it smelled stale and took an eternity to go up a mere seven floors. A pale-yellow colored hallway with a long, skinny wooden table on one side. Dusty, fake plants in a wicker basket sitting on top. Doors on either side of the hall. Different offices for different companies. At the end of the hall, a larger polished oak door. Behind it, a raised reception desk with an open entryway on either side. Both leading to an open space of office cubicles. The outer wall glass and covered with floor-to-ceiling mini-blinds. Grey painted doors every ten feet or so divide them, framed prints of high-rise buildings in between them. These are doors to other small offices. The last one on the right. I know this office. Inside it, the walls are painted a dull grayish-green color. It's well lit, yet a small fluorescent desk lamp stays on to light up the desk. There's a black leather chair with a small rip that clings to my slacks. A cork-board on the wall has a hand-drawn floor-plan pinned to it with old-school, flat metal thumbtacks. It's the floor-plan of my house. I remember being in this office on this day. It was time for me to go. I looked at my watch. If we don't go soon, we'll still be stuck there when the shops at the marketplace close. The marketplace, it's a farmer's market of sorts. I remember. When it closes, the streets get jammed with all the exiting traffic. We want to avoid the traffic, but who is *we?* There's a window. I'm looking out. Waiting for something. Someone. I can see the main road out there. Cars zip past, looking miniature from way up here. Then I see it. A black car. A convertible. It's turning off of the main road, riding up the side street into the back entrance parking lot. The driver parks close to the building. The driver's door opens and a woman steps out. I can't see her very well from up here. She's out of her car, walking towards the building. She's wearing a light colored blouse and a light blue skirt. Her shoulder length hair is dark brown, almost black. She looks back at the car as she holds up the remote key to lock the car. When she turns back toward the building, I see her face. She's smiling. She's beautiful. I feel joy and sadness overwhelming me at the same time. I love her. I'm certain of that. I miss her. I'm certain of that too. This is her. This is the other woman.

Rolling over on my side, I realize that I wasn't actually sleeping. I was just remembering. In my mind's eye, I was riding that elevator, walking down those halls, sitting in that office. I was remembering things from my life. This was real. Not a dream. The woman, she's the one from my dream. I have to figure out a way to find her. I don't see how that's even possible. I don't even know her name. I have to find out, somehow. Rolling over onto my back, I start to think of any way. Any way that I might be able to figure this out. To see her. The marketplace. I need to find out what the marketplace is, and where it is. Maybe that will jog my memory. I'm lost in that thought when I eventually do fall asleep.

The dreams come. This time disjointed. Flashing images. Confusing. Scary. A postcard of a hotel on a sunny beach. The postcard bursts into flames. A child's laughter, somehow menacing and evil. My father's voice yelling something I can't make out. Then silence, and softly, a woman's voice whispering in my ear, "Please...come back to me." It's not Lisa's voice. I think it must be her. The other woman. A familiar song plays. It's a theme song to a sitcom, yet I can't remember which one. Silence again. I'm sitting at a picnic table. It's old and worn. I see wildflowers. Bright blue and in every direction. I'm not alone. The woman is here with me. She's across from me, unpacking the contents of a small canvas bag on the table. Wine, cheese, and crackers. She's wearing a white flowing long sleeve shirt, her long dark hair flipping in the wind. She looks angelic in the sunlight.

"Take a picture," she says, handing me a cheap disposable camera from her bag.

I walk a few feet from the table and turn back toward her. She pivots her head, putting her hand on her cheek in a mock pose. Then she changes poses to look right at the camera, with a hint of a smile on her lips. Her face. I know that face.

"I think I might cut my hair," she proclaims. "How do I look?"

"Like my fiancé," I reply.

"Well, that's because I am, silly."

Just as I snap the picture, looking through the camera viewfinder, I realize it. This is the exact frame. This is it. The picture of the old picnic table from the photo album.

"OH, honey. You're sweating like crazy." Lisa's voice.

I open my eyes and she's standing over the bed with a tray in hand.

"I was bringing you soup," she says. "But maybe not the best meal with you being all hot and sweaty."

I have lost all track of time. It feels like the middle of the night.

"I'm okay. Just give me a moment." Sitting up I look over at her. "Soup sounds fine."

She sets the tray down on the bed.

"Are you sure, babe? I can make something else."

I feel the guilt crawling in again. I feel like I must stink of it. I can't imagine that Lisa doesn't smell it too.

"No, no. Really. Soup sounds good, actually." I slide the tray up closer to me, studying her face for a moment. I realize she's not suspicious. She's sad.

"What time is it?" I ask.

"It's almost seven." Mentioning as she looks down at her watch.

I start to ask if she means in the morning or night, but I can see through the crack in the curtains that it's nighttime. I know she wants to know what I remember. If I remember her.

"You know," I begin. "I'm getting more and more memories back each day. I really am."

"That's great, babe. Really." Almost trying to convince herself, it seems.

I can tell she's hopeful, but she's afraid to ask if I remember her. I'm half tempted to lie and say that I do. My emotions continue their seemingly endless battle. I feel like I have to choose to either take care of my own needs, or hers. What can I say to give her hope? Should I give her hope at all? Should I abandon all hope of finding this other woman? The last answer is easy. Of course I should, yet I know deep down that I have no real choice. I must find her. I have to get out of this house again.

It is then that I think of something that will likely bring up Lisa's spirits and also get me out of this house.

"I know it probably sounds crazy," I say. "But I think it would be good for us to get out of this house together. As a family. Maybe spend the day doing something fun. Maybe it'll help me to remember things."

"Wow," she says, but I can't tell if it's a positive response or not. "That would be great." She smiles, and I realize that my suggestion also tells her that I still do not remember her.

"How about tomorrow?" I suggest.

"Sure." Sounding a bit less enthusiastic than I would have expected. "Let me think about where...but, yeah. It'll be fun." Again, almost dryly. She's hurt, and I can't do anything to prevent it.

"Cool," I reply, staring into my soup.

I start eating in silence. She's looking off into space.

"Okay, I've got to go finish up some chores." She stands and abruptly walks out and down the hall.

She is hurt, of that I'm certain. But she's also growing colder towards me. I can feel it. I don't know if I blame her, considering what I must have done to her. To our family. Nevertheless, I know what I feel about this other woman. I cannot deny my feelings for her, I simply can't. My fiancé? In my dream, I called her my fiancé. Was it a memory? Were we planning to get married? How could I be when I'm already married? Was I planning to divorce Lisa? Is that why she is keeping things from me? Deep down, I know that Lisa will say and do whatever it takes to keep me here. To keep me away from this other woman. A wild chain of thoughts run through my brain. What if Lisa isn't my wife? What if this other woman is, and Lisa is hiding that from me? Then I think of Tyler, and the house, the dog, the doctor...the endless string of little details that make that impossible. I realize that I'm now really starting to think like a paranoid madman. I have to keep reality in check, but I know there is something big being hidden from me here. I can't fully trust Lisa until I know what that is.

12

Surprisingly, I fall asleep again soon after eating. I half wonder if she put something in the soup. More thoughts of a paranoid madman. I know that I cannot trust everything she tells me, but I don't think she's capable of drugging me. My body just needs more rest than it's been getting. The night goes by without any dreams, except that I keep thinking I hear a beeping, whirring noise. The noise of machinery, like a computer or something. Every time I sit up to really try to listen closely, it seems to fade away.

Lisa wakes me up early.

"Rise and shine, sleepy head. Breakfast is ready, and then we're off to spend the day together." Sounding much more cheery than she was last night. I'm glad to hear she's warming up to the idea of a family outing, yet I'm distracted by yet another morning with no memory of her or Tyler. My hopes of ever remembering them are shrinking with the start of each day.

"There's a place we've talked about going several times. It's like a science center. They have lots of exhibits, and even a few aquariums. I think it'll be a good balance of fun for us and for

Tyler. Plus, it sits on the bay, so maybe we can have lunch on the water while we are there," she offers.

"Sounds nice." Thinking that it really does.

"Great. Let's get you up and fed then." She leans in to kiss me. I lean in and kiss her back. It feels acted out. Staged. I'm wishing I had not had sex with her on our first night back here. We have had very little physical contact since then, and that is starting to hang thick in the air. She's made a big breakfast of scrambled eggs, crispy bacon, fried potatoes and sautéed onion slices. It's delicious and we eat without saying much. Quiet breakfasts seem to be our thing. Even Tyler is quiet this morning. He stares at me through most of breakfast, not returning a smile when I send him one. Is he realizing I don't remember who he is? No, I'm being paranoid again. He's only four. I finish my breakfast, and head for the shower. I've gotten pretty good at functioning with one hand, including showering and keeping my cast dry. Tucking my towel over the shower door handle, I peel off my clothes, still careful of my arm. Naked, I pass the mirror and stop to take a good look at myself. I look tired, older. I have been sleeping a lot, yet I've still got dark circles under my eyes. The bandage on my forehead looking worn and dirty. Lisa tells me I have to leave it on until my upcoming appointment with Dr. Lambert. It's really just an extra large Band-Aid. It hasn't hurt in a while. I decide to peel it up a bit, just to see how my head looks underneath. The glue around the edge of the bandage sticks hard to my skin, and it pinches when I start to pull it up. I move slowly, trying not to hurt the skin or ruin the bandage. I need to be able to stick it back on. Looking in the mirror, peeling the bandage back, I study the skin underneath as it's revealed. It looks...fine. Perfectly fine. Not so much as a scab. Not even a scrape. There is literally no sign of any injury on my head. Peeling the bandage almost all the way off, I see dark stains on the underside of it, as if my head had previously bled underneath. Then, I notice something. The stain is neon blue. It's not red or brown, like old dried blood should be. Peeling off the last bit of it, I hold the bandage out in front of me and look at the blue stain. It's not a stain. It's writing. In blue marker, written in perfectly scribed backwards letters, it reads "COME BACK TO ME" with a little hand drawn heart, and I instantly know who the message is from. The woman. But how could...?

"You getting in the shower, Mr. Man? We need to get going." Lisa, opening the bedroom door and walking in. I look to the bathroom door and note that it's slightly ajar. I fumble with the bandage. It slips from my hand and lands on the floor. Lisa is almost to the bathroom door now. I drop to my knees, searching for it. It's stuck to the rug. Lisa pushes on the bathroom door, it starts to open. I pull the bandage off the rug and toss it into the toilet, then quickly sit down over it.

"You okay in there?" She pushes back on the door, glancing in.

"I'm on the toilet." Modesty lacing my voice, hoping we have some level of privacy established.

"Yikes. Sorry. Maybe close the bathroom door next time?" I hear her say as she walks back out of the bedroom.

I sit there a moment, getting my racing heart to slow down. That was close, and I wonder how she would have reacted if she saw the note. The lack of any injury on my forehead is much less important to me than determining how this other woman could have gotten to the underside of my bandage to leave a message. Was she in the house? Did she do this in the hospital?... and why is it written backwards? Did she expect me to see it in a mirror? In any case, she is looking for me, and she is trying to prevent Lisa from finding out. This gives me hope that I will find her. If she knows my situation, then she must know how difficult it is going to be. I will find her. I flush the bandage down the toilet and get into the shower.

. . .

"You weren't supposed to take that bandage off, but your head does look all healed up." Lisa doesn't seem upset that I've removed it. A good sign.

We pull out of the driveway, heading to a place called Discovery Bay. She's described it as a sort of science exhibition. We're in my truck again, since her car is still in the shop. Tyler is all strapped up in a booster seat in the back, thumbing through a children's book, strangely quiet again.

"Yeah, I don't see any sign of an injury. Like, not even the faintest scar," I say.

"Well, it wasn't a huge gash or anything to begin with, but the doctor certainly did a great job," she responds.

A great job? A Band-Aid? I think, but don't say. If it was just a scratch, why tell me not to take of the bandage for a week? Why the headaches?

"I suppose so. Seems like less of an injury than I expected. No stitches or anything. I'm surprised there isn't at least a scab or something. The bandage seemed kind of overkill for a little scratch," I reply.

"Well, it looks great. Don't be cynical," she replies.

Approaching the neighborhood gate, it opens and we head left. The same way we came in from the hospital. The same way I went on the bike. Cresting the hill, I look to my right, toward the shopping center I'd visited on the bike. Except, it's not there. In its place, a huge field of blue flowers. We pass a sign that reads 'Acorn Park' and underneath: 'Picnicking. Pavilions. Swimming. Canoe Rentals.' I start to take a deep breath in through my nose, trying not to panic. We pass the park and continue past wooded areas on both sides of the road. Up and down and a few more hills, the road starts making a subtle bend to the right. We pass several entryways to other neighborhoods. The road straightens back out and there it is, on my right. The shopping center. The home repair store. The gas station. Immediately past that, the entry to the grocery store's parking lot. We are probably ten miles from the entrance to our neighborhood. I didn't think I biked this far. I don't recall passing a park, or other neighborhoods. This just confirms what I've been trying to come to terms with since the accident. I simply cannot rely on my own view of things. In my head, I list out the strange things I've been experiencing, and I realize that I truly am lost. I don't trust Lisa. I cannot trust myself. I have no doubt that something inside my brain is damaged and malfunctioning. I have no way of knowing what is real and what is not. That distant life raft of hope floating further out to sea, then sinking out of sight. I think I would rather die than live like this forever. Then I realize that the note on the bandage might not have been real. The dreams. All products of my damaged brain trying to put my life back together.

But there is one thing I know to be real. The other woman. I can't explain why I know this. I just do. The emotions I feel when I see her in my head are very real. But everything else...all of these things I think I remember, the little details...I know that these are possibly just made up in my head. Even if I found this woman now, it would never be the same between us again. I'm brain damaged now, maybe permanently. I feel a tear leap down my face.

"Oh no! What's wrong? Are you okay?" Genuine concern in Lisa's voice.

Despite my mistrust of her, I'm unable to keep it all in. "I'm okay. I just...I have thoughts that I know aren't real."

Lowering my voice so Tyler doesn't hear me, I whisper, "Things that don't make sense. Impossible things. I think I need to see the doctor again soon. Like, really soon."

She stays calm, which surprises me again. She puts her hand

on my knee. "Oh, babe, the doctor explained that something like this might happen."

"Wait. What? He did?" I ask.

"Yes, and he told me to pay close attention to your moods," she explains.

"Why wouldn't he tell me this directly? Why wouldn't you tell me this?" I ask.

"Because he did not want to scare you. I don't want to scare you either."

I'm sitting here, stunned. She didn't want to scare me? Did she think that my experiencing these things without knowing they are normal would be less scary?

"Steve, the results from all of your tests came back fine. But they want to follow up because sometimes complications like this arise a little while after incidents like yours. People get disoriented. There are all kinds of possible symptoms. For example, experiencing more 'lost' time, ringing in the ears, replacing one memory for another. There's a slew of other examples." She continues. "I could tell that you weren't being totally honest with me, and maybe you don't trust me because you can't remember us, but I only want you to heal. To get better."

I wince at her saying aloud that I do not remember them, looking back at Tyler, his face still buried in the book. "Hey. Can you not say that in front of him?" I ask.

"Fine." She talk-whispers. "But he knows something is up, babe. He can tell. He's asked me if you still love him." Her eyes go all wet.

"I'm sorry. I truly am. How do you think I feel? It's like I'm destroying my family and myself at the same time. I'm trapped in here." I point to my head.

"You should have told me that the doctor said this. I've been feeling like I'm going crazy. Like I'm trying to figure out some impossible equation." As I go on, I realize I'm getting louder.

"I can imagine it's really scary, but what you're experiencing isn't unexpected from someone who has been through what you have."

"Isn't unexpected?" I reply. "So, it's perfectly normal to hear footsteps and voices in your house when no one is there. It's normal to see light in your eyes when there isn't really anything there. Oh, and maybe the doctor should have told me that side effects from head injury may include having conversations with your dead father," I say, and I realize I'm almost yelling.

"You...you've been speaking to your dad?" She asks, and I notice the look on her face. There's no mistaking it. She looks threatened.

"Yes, I have, and I've seen him too. I've seen him standing right in front of me." Suddenly aware of what I've been saying, I lower my voice and glance back at Tyler. He's looking out the window, as if he can't even hear us. Maybe he's trying not to.

"Well, you didn't tell me that." She states, now with a hint of concern in her voice. "We should definitely contact the doctor when we get back home and see what he thinks. Until then, I think we should try not to worry."

"Yeah, I know. I mean, I do know that and you're right. But even if the doctor said that visions of dead relatives are expected, which he won't, that won't cure the fact that I wake up every day hoping my memory is back. I have to start facing the possibility that my memory may never come back. That I might have to start all over here." I say, and now I'm the one getting louder. "Maybe a possibility that you should consider too."

She sniffles, then blinks, and her tears go away. Looking out at the road, she calmly says, "Start all over with or without us, Steve?"

"With you, of course. You two are my family," I say, not knowing if I even mean it.

"Well then, that's all I need to know. I will stand by your side through this. I will be there for you. I will do whatever it takes. Whatever it takes to bring you back to us. I won't give up on you. Don't give up on us." She smiles. A gentle, loving smile.

"I won't."

And even as the words leave my lips, they feel like another lie.

13

E xiting the interstate, Lisa turns onto a side street and stops at the traffic light. The silence in the truck is suffocating. There's tension between us, yet I have no way of extinguishing it. At least not without lying. Nothing looks familiar here. A few low-rise office buildings. An empty baseball field. The light turns green and we take an immediate right, Lisa seems to know this route well. She hasn't referenced anything for directions. Taking a left at the next light, she pulls under a "Discovery Bay" sign overhead and into a large, open parking lot. There's a great big building off to one side of it. It's a huge, dome shaped building with a metallic sign above the front door that reads "Discovery Bay. Learn. Play. Discover." The parking lot and the building site edge right up to the bay, which makes for an amazing view for visitors. Several boats are scattered throughout the deep blue water. It's beautiful here and it gives me a twinge of optimism. Whether I remember anything more or not today, the walking and the fresh air will be good for me. Good for us. The parking lot is packed, and it takes a few minutes to find a space. By the time we park, I'm feeling better and it seems as though the cloud of tension between Lisa and I have dissipated.

As we climb out of the truck, I reflect on my initial intention in suggesting a day out together. If I'm honest with myself, it was really just so I could get out of that house, but our discussion on the way has me rethinking my intentions. Do I really suspect there's some sort of conspiracy between Lisa and Tyler to trick me into a life that's not really what we had before? No, that's ludicrous. If I keep thinking like a crazy person, then that's exactly what I'll become. Knowing that Lisa was aware that I might experience these strange side-effects, or whatever they are, doesn't help me to feel like I can trust her. Internally, I commit, yet again, to stop trying to figure everything out and just take in the day. But I know that, even if it stops happening, I must understand why I have seen and heard things that aren't real. If there is a scientific reason for even one of these occurrences, as Lisa suggests, I want to know what it is. I find myself almost anticipating the next hallucination, or whatever clinical term might be more correct for these events. An older man in a brown trench coat walks past the truck. Is he real, or my imagination? Yes, he's real. But I could play these games with myself for everything and everyone I encounter.

Again, my thoughts shift for a moment to this other woman, whomever she is. I know that I've had some sort of a relationship with her. I can feel that much. Regardless of what tricks my mind might be playing on me as a result of the accident, I know that she is real. As much as I'd like to forget about her and move on with my life now, I must find out who she is, if for no other reason than to put it to rest. Part of me feels that if I know the truth, I can let it go. Perhaps it's the mystery of all of it that has me romanticizing about this unknown relationship with her. Maybe it would be easy to leave alone if she wasn't asking me to find her, if she hadn't left a seemingly impossible secret message for me. As I'm telling myself all of these 'what-ifs', I know it's all bullshit. I know I love this woman. I'm sure of that, if nothing else.

I close my eyes for just a moment. I have to take it one day at a time. Today, I'm with Lisa and Tyler. My family. Whatever I have done—whatever Lisa is hiding—this is still my family. Opening my eyes, I look at her for a moment. I am going to commit to try to be present with them right here, right now. To let myself remain ignorant of what might really be happening to me. Continuing to focus on all the mysteries and the unknowns feels like it's going to drive me insane.

On the walk up to the entry building, Tyler catches up to me and asks if I will carry him. I wonder if he's warming back up to me.

"Dad only has one good arm right now, baby," Lisa warns. "He can't carry you just yet."

"No, no, I can do it." I say. "I just need a little help getting him up and down."

Lisa smiles at me. "Are you sure?"

"Positive," I say.

She puts down her bag, and lifts Tyler up to my right arm. I hold him up against me. He's heavier than I expected. Another pang of guilt hits me. I can't help but wonder what this must be like for him. I can only hope that he doesn't know that I don't remember him. Does he think his own father's feeling for him might have changed? Can he sense something like that? I want to tell him that everything is going to be okay...that I love him. But how could I lie to him like that? I don't know him. How could I love him? Looking at him now, in my arm, one of his little arms is holding onto me around the back of my neck, I think that I could grow into loving this boy. He needs me, and I need to be here for him. We head inside the building to the front lobby. The attendant, an old woman with a scowl on her face, takes our payment for tickets and snaps plastic wristbands on each of us. He snaps mine a little too tight, and as I try to adjust it, I notice that it looks just like the kind you get at the hospital. For a fleeting moment, it reminds me again of what's happened, so I quickly dismiss that thought and focus on this moment with Tyler and Lisa as I told myself I'd do. We pass through the lobby and head inside the main exhibit hall. As soon as the exhibits come into view, Tyler wants down to run off to whatever has caught his attention so I squat down to let him go.

"Stay where we can see you!" Lisa yells after him, as he runs over to the first exhibit. It's some sort of interactive computer display that plays music. She grabs my hand and walks me toward an exhibit on the opposite side of the room. Banks of laser lights dance along the wall. She stops me at the wall, turns to me and kisses me on the cheek.

"You are going to have fun today, even if it kills you," she says.

She looks so serious for a moment that it actually scares me. Then, she cracks a big warm smile. I feel a stir of affection for her.

"This place does look neat." I comment, turning around in a wide circle.

"Yes, it does. We're going to have to drag Tyler out of here." She points in his direction, looking across the room at him.

"Hey." I stand directly in front of her for moment, making sure she's looking at me. "I'm sorry if I wigged out on the way here. It's just that... "

"Stop." She interrupts my sentence. "There's absolutely no reason for you to apologize. I'm the one who should be apologizing. You are right. I should have told you. I really thought it would be best to wait and see if you had any of these symptoms, and I thought that mentioning them to you ahead of time would scare you. I didn't want you anticipating something that might not even happen."

I have to admit, it makes sense. Her wanting to protect me

from unnecessary fear. I'm struck with more guilt for not trusting her. I want this all to end. I want to be able to fully open up to her.

"I see." I reach up and run my good hand through her hair for a moment. "I can see why you'd think keeping it from me was a good idea, and I appreciate you trying to help me, but I need to know. I need to be aware of everything so I can assess things from my perspective too. My not knowing things is making me...well, it's making me suspicious. What you said in the truck about my being paranoid and not trusting you, I hate it, babe, but...you are right. I'm struggling with that, and I need your help."

"How can I help you to trust me when I can't help you remember me?" she asks, and her eyes pool up with tears. It touches my heart and I feel something for her. Love?

"But, regardless, you are right too." She continues. "I should have said something, and *I'm* sorry. I'm sorry if my not telling you made you question your own sanity, or made you feel lost and alone."

Looking intently into my eyes, she says, "You're not alone. You'll never be alone."

Again, her last sentence sounds menacing to me, and it sends an uncomfortable feeling crawling over my skin. She's apologizing, and trying to make me feel better. Why am I already so untrusting of her again? What has happened to me? I close my eyes for a moment, intentionally breaking the connection between her eyes and mine. I don't really know how to respond but the awkwardness of the moment is growing by the second by my not responding at all.

"Well, thank you for saying that," I reply. "You can help me actually, and I can help you to help me. We can do this by just agreeing to be honest with each other. I think that's the key to us moving through all of this together."

"You mean, to moving *past* all of it," she adds.

"Yes. To moving past it." I agree.

"Agreed." She leans in to kiss me. I give her a quick peck on the lips and it still feels like I'm kissing a stranger.

Looking past me, she scans for Tyler. He's still sitting at the computer display, pushing buttons with both hands. As if he can tell I'm looking at him too, he stops and looks straight at me for a moment. His face frozen in a blank, emotionless, dead stare. It makes me uncomfortable and I look away.

Turning my attention to where we are standing, in front of us a stack of multicolored light-beams reach from one partition wall to another. I reach my good hand across them. As I touch each one, it plays a slightly different tune than the one before it.

"Serenading me?" She teases.

"I remember now. I was once a world-class musician," I joke back.

"Now I know your memory is whacked," she says, playfully jabbing a finger at my ribs.

"Ow! That's my sore side!" I say.

"Oh no. I'm so sorry!" She expresses, suddenly serious.

"It's actually the other side," I say, grinning.

"Oh, you are a brat!" She laughs, taking my hand.

I squeeze it, and she squeezes back. I want this to be real. I want to trust her. I want this other woman to be a figment of my imagination. I want to just forget about her, and the visions, and move on with my life now with my wife. The nagging feeling that I'm being lied to; that something is being hidden from me... it continues to tug at the recesses of my brain, like an anchor weighing me down to a place in my past that I cannot remember.

"Wow. This one is cool!" Lisa says, bringing me back to this moment.

We've walked around the curved wall of the room, Tyler still on the far side playing with the computers. This next exhibit has bins of colored golf balls on both sides. Miniature plastic slides intertwine down different ramps ending in a black box labeled 'music machine'. Apparently, each colored ball makes a different note when it enters the machine. Guests can drop the balls into holes that send them down the different ramps and make music from it, or something like that. Lisa starts feeding in golf balls, as they zigzag down the ramps in to the black box, dropping in one at a time, making a sort of melody.

"Not bad. Not bad," I say. She laughs.

"Okay, you're turn." She points to the pile of golf balls.

Instead of carefully placing them on each slide, I pile as many as I can on three of the slides, just to be playful. As the line of balls start entering the machine, they start making different tones. The tones start coming out as individual sounds, then as patterns. Eventually, the patterns start alternating into another melody. Wait..it's making a song. I know this song. In my head, I scan for the name of it.

"Mmmm. Dudada da da..." I hum aloud, trying to remember the song. How did I even make an actual existing song with this thing?

Then, a few words come to me. "Girl, it's you and me, like the waves upon the sea," I sing aloud.

I look over at Lisa, and her face is one of pure terror.

Suddenly, pictures flash in my mind, like a slideshow running at full speed. I barely have time to see an image before the next one comes. Blood splattering into a fine mist of red dots on a white surface. Multi-colored coins flipping through the air. I hear someone screaming, the grinding of teeth.

"Are you okay?" Lisa, now holding my arms.

I look around and note that I'm still standing by the ball-slide machine. The music has stopped. Looking back at Lisa, she's intensely staring at me. What the hell were those visions?

More random side effects? Why did she look so scared? No more than ten minutes after proclaiming that honesty is the key to moving past this, I lie again.

"I'm totally fine. Why?" I ask.

"Oh..." she responds, letting go of my arms. "You just seemed...like you were in a trance or something for a second there," she says. "Were you singing?"

Her inquisition seems so much more than just the caring for a loved one. So much different, as if she's investigating something, or fishing for answers, just like me.

"Nah...I was just goofing around." I tell her. "Let's check the rest of this place out."

As we make our way back around the room to Tyler, I try to remember what I saw or what I heard. It was so fast; I can't really tell what it was. Blood? Paint? Was someone screaming or... maybe just singing? The intensity of the images diminish by the second, and I'm actually feeling normal again by the time we get to Tyler, or...as normal as I can be anymore.

Tyler is jumping back and forth on oversized drum pads on the floor. Each jump making a different drum sound. Looking over at us in between jumps, he's got a huge smile on his face. It's contagious, and I smile back. It feels good to know that he's happy. It makes me happy. I can't help myself, and I jump in, bouncing from pad to pad in between him. They are spongy, like mini trampolines. Tyler and I bounce back and forth past each other, making a horrible racket. He starts cracking up and his laughter makes me feel better.

Abruptly, Lisa suggests we check out another room. Tyler was having such fun that I'd expected him to resist, but instead, he races through the passageway into the next room. We quicken our pace to catch up to him. As we walk in, I'm winded from the drumpad jumping sessions. Looking around, I notice that this room is huge compared to the first one. It's like a massive open-ceiling warehouse with two floors. Exhibits are placed in seemingly random locations all along both floors. A big plastic sign in the middle reads: 'The Science Of Your Body'. There's a huge open-mouth sculpture with a walkway through it, aimed at teaching kids about the importance of healthy teeth. This place is crawling with kids. There must be hundreds of them. We walk past a towering statue of a man with a transparent plastic bubble in place of his stomach—an exhibit on how the human digestive system works. Looking up to the second floor railing, I see an exhibit with an oversized plastic human brain. That one hits too close to home and I decide to avoid it.

Tyler sprints up the stairs and Lisa runs after him.

"Tyler! Slow down!" She calls to him, then looks back at me.

"You go ahead! I'm still winded from jumping, " I say, smiling "I need a rest. I'll catch up in a few minutes."

She waves and then disappears upstairs. I take a few minutes to fully catch my breath, slowly wandering around a small section of the first floor, just below the stairs Lisa and Tyler just raced up. Walking past a few exhibits swarming with kids, one of a burping machine, another of a plastic running nose. In front of me, a huge structure shaped like a human heart. Passages lead in and out of it, like caves. There's even a slide out of one side, down through one of the valves. I walk into the first heart passage. I take a few turns in the crisscrossing tunnels and end up right where I started, or so I think. I'm starting to feel a little lost in here. The exhibit wasn't all that big from the outside, so I must be walking in circles. I notice the exit signs above and start following them. I wonder why there aren't other people in this exhibit, especially with all the kids in this place. Now I notice that I am, in fact, back where I started and the feeling of being lost goes away. Even with the dimly lit, cave-like passages, the detail is an impressive array of tiny purple veins.

They look so real. As I reach out to touch one of the walls, I hear her.

"Please don't be scared," she says, almost incoherently, except to her intended recipient.

I spin toward her voice. It's so familiar.

"Who's there?" I say, scanning the dimness of the passage in front of me.

"Oh, Steve, I miss you so much. I know you are trying. I know you are. I can just tell. But I need you to come back to me. I need you to find me again," she says. I smell perfume. A hint of jasmine.

Then, I know. It's her. The woman from my dreams. My memories. She said 'Find me again'. I think of the bandage.

"Who are you?" I say.

"Steve, it's me. It's Haley. I love you." She says, as I feel goose-bumps raise on my arms with this revelation of her name.

Haley. The name floods my brain with memories. College graduation. A fancy party. Champagne. Everyone wearing tuxedos and dresses. A hotel room surrounded by snow-covered mountains. The dog, Annie. Something's not right. I can feel myself starting to pass out. I take a deep breath, slow, in through my nose, out through my mouth. Sliding down to my knees, I hold myself up against one of the veiny cave walls. Another deep breath. Then another. My heart beating a thousand beats a minute, how appropriate for where I find myself in this heart exhibit. Slowly, I stand back up. Using all of my willpower, I step toward her voice. I here her footsteps, shuffling away. Breaking into a run, I almost fall taking the next corner of the cave. Then, I see her. Walking quickly into another passage. She looks back at me and I see her face. It is her. Haley. She looks just like she did in the office parking lot. In my memory. My dream? My emotions hit me harder than the memories. I am in love with her. I slow down a bit to squeeze past a plump little kid, then follow her into the next passage. It slopes uphill and I start to run again when the passage abruptly turns. Around the corner, it leads to a low tunnel. The slide. The exit. Careful of my arm, I sit and slide down, exiting the exhibit. There she is, walking quickly out of one of the building's exit doors. I hurry to catch up, slowed by a family blocking the doorway with a stroller. Shuffling past, I almost run right into two little, curly-headed girls holding hands. I skip around them, rushing through the exit door and out into the parking lot. The sun is temporarily blinding and for a moment, I can't see anything. I squint to scan the lot and see no sign of her. She's gone. Running out into the parking lot, I try to look in every direction at once. On the verge of giving up, I see the car. A black convertible Mini Cooper. I know that car. It's the car she was driving the day that she drove to the office building. Running toward the car, it backs out of its spot, then takes off toward the exit.

"Wait!" I try to yell out, but it's no use. She's too far away.

She stops at the light. Just as I think I might actually catch up to her, the light changes and she starts to accelerate. She hesitates, and looks over at me. I see her lips moving but I'm too far away to hear what she's saying, but I can tell that she's crying. Pushing my legs as hard as I can, I run full speed towards her. I hold my good arm out with my index finger up, in a gesture for her to wait a moment. I'm maybe twenty feet from the car now. Still crying, she blows me a kiss with her left hand. I notice a wedding ring on it.

"I can't do this without you. Come back to me." She yells. Her car takes off and is out of my sight before I reach the light, my legs collapsing under me.

THEN, nothing. Black. Silent.

14

"Steve. Can you hear me?" I know that voice. The grey-toothed doctor.

It's Dr. Bowden. As I remember this, it dawns on me that my memory seems to work fine regarding people and events that have happened since I fell, just not those from before it. I open my eyes and everything is blurry for a moment. I'm in a bed, back in the hospital. A different room this time. Smaller. A curtain wraps around half of the room. Under it, I see the bottom of another bed. A shared room. There stands the same doctor, glasses still perched up on his head.

"I can hear you." I look his way.

"Thank God! Oh, thank God! You're awake. Do you remember what happened?" Lisa's voice. I look over and see her standing on the other side of the bed.

"Yes. No. Well, kind of." I state, my confusion evident in my voice.

"You fell again, although it appears that you did not hit your head this time. We're all lucky for that," the doctor explains.

I do remember. Haley. The car. I remember starting to pass out.

"What were you doing outside the science center?" Lisa asks. She sounds genuinely worried.

I pause, thinking of what to say. "I just got a little claustrophobic with all of the kids in there. I stepped out for some fresh air."

"Why were you all the way out in the parking lot? You were almost out in the road." She questions, with a hint of annoyance in her voice.

"I...I don't know. I remember going for a walk." I lie.

"A walk? Why would you leave us there and go for a walk?" Her voice escalating from mild annoyance, now starting to sound aggravated.

"Let's. Just. Take this slow," the doctor suggests. "I assume you remember me then? Dr. Bowen?"

"Yes, I remember you." Saying this, I see the pain on Lisa's face. Something I have yet to say to her.

"Steve, how do you feel?" I want to respond that physically, I feel fine. Mentally is an entirely different answer.

I close my eyes, surveying my body. No aches. No pains. My head still feels fine. My arm doesn't even hurt.

"I feel fine. Better than I can remember feeling since the fall. The first one." I reiterate.

"That's good, Steve. That's good. I want you be aware of where we are at at this moment in time." Looking down at his chart—my chart—he glances back up to me.

"At this moment in time? What do you mean? How long have I been in here?" I ask.

"Only a few hours...You were dehydrated, and I'd initially suspected you simply passed out from pushing yourself too hard. But, we've run a few more tests, the results leading us to more closely examine a few sections of the original tests." Glancing back down at my file, I anxiously await his continuation.

"And?" I ask.

"Well, you were scheduled to meet with the neurology specialist later this week, Dr. Lambert. You recall?"

"Yes. I know," I say.

He continues. "But, given the incident today, I called him directly. Coincidentally, he was actually in town seeing another patient. He came down here straight away to see you."

"What did he say?" I ask, wanting to cut to the chase.

"Well, I would rather he discuss the intricate details with you directly. But, we think we know what's happened to you. Why you fell originally. Why you can't remember some things but can others. You see, Dr. Lambert has discovered something that... well, frankly...that we missed. We think that your memory loss isn't a result of your initial fall. Rather, the fall was likely caused by the same thing that is actually causing your memory loss." He takes a deep breath before continuing on.

"Dr. Lambert has found a small blockage in your brain. Specifically, a part of Hippocampus. This is the part of the brain responsible for memories. A loss of memory is common with this type of blockage," he says.

"Blockage." The panic in my voice evident. "What is it? A tumor?"

"Not likely. Most often these types of scenarios derive from a benign cyst. A build up of tissue." Taking his glasses off his head, he faces me eye to eye.

"Is that typically...curable? I mean, can they remove the blockage?" I ask.

He holds his glasses up to his mouth, breathes on them, then wipes the lenses with the bottom of his coat. "We are discussing options, but yes, typically that is one of them."

Perching his glasses back up on his head. It makes me wonder why he cleaned them at all.

"See, when the brain suffers this kind of blockage, symptoms almost always include memory loss. Other problems can include dizziness, which would explain your initial fall. It's also important to note that, in these types of situations, many memories come back on their own. Typically, the oldest come back first, then the newer ones."

"That might explain why I can't remember..." I start to say, looking at Lisa.

"Yes." She answers for him, looking on. "Dr. Bowen and I have talked about that. We are in agreement that it could be why you don't remember me."

The doctor takes a pause. I reflect for a moment on what it might be like to have to undergo brain surgery. I'm not scared of that. I'm only scared of continuing to live like this. Scared of seeing and hearing things that aren't there. Whatever it takes to change that, I'm all for it. I want a normal life. Most of all, I want to remember. I want to remember everything.

"So, what are these options?" I ask.

"Well, we can monitor your status, keeping an eye on the blockage, and see if you make a full recovery. Sometimes, the effects of these types of blockages go away on their own, making it harmless in the long run." He points out. "Another option would be to attempt to remove the blockage. There is certainly risk with this option, but..." he continues.

I interrupt. "What do you mean by full recovery? What advantage is there in removing the blockage? Is it dangerous to leave it there? Is it more likely that I'll get all my memories back with it removed?"

"One thing at a time, Steve. Removing the blockage won't magically give you your memories back, no. But it could smoothen, and possibly accelerate the process. Keep in mind that it may have no affect on your memories at all. That's not the main reason we are considering removal." He reflects, affording me the uneasiness of knowing that there's more to this blockage than what they want to disclose.

I look at Lisa then back at the doctor, suddenly aware of the seriousness on both of their faces. Something is wrong with me. Something bigger than previously thought.

"Why then?" I ask.

"The blockage is likely the reason you passed out and fell to begin with. Now that this has happened again, we have to consider the risk in leaving the blockage there. You could pass out in the shower, or while driving," he says.

"Doctor..." I pause. I have to tell him about the things I've seen. I don't want Lisa to know. "Can I talk with you alone for a moment?" I look at Lisa.

The look on Lisa's face at my request speaks volumes.

"What? Anything going on with you is my business as much as it is anyone's." Standing, she anxiously glances between me and him. "Why would you want to keep me from hearing what you have to say, Steve?" She continues looking back and forth between the doctor and me, similar to watching a tennis match between two players who show no signs of giving up. "Oh, I get it. The paranoia thing. The 'I can't trust this woman because I don't remember her even though she is my fucking wife' thing?!" She's getting louder.

I knew she'd be hurt by my request for privacy, especially after our talk of honesty, but I'm stunned by just how suddenly and extremely her demeanor changes. It leaves me speechless for a few moments.

"Let's all just take a moment here," Dr. Bowen says.

"Fuck that. I've done everything I can to try and help him. To be there. He remembers everyone but me. But me AND his own son!" She points her finger in my face.

"Maybe it's on purpose. Maybe you don't want to remember!" She looks at me, her eyes enraged, full of tears. "Maybe you don't want to remember what you did to me. To us. Well, let me tell you something, Mr. Lewis. You fucked us over. That's what you did. You fucked me and Tyler over, and..." She trails off, getting softer. "You fucked her over too."

"Everyone's emotions are on high right now, but..." The doctor starts.

"No." She says. Her voice remaining softer. "It's fine. I'll go, but remember this, Steve. I have always been here for you, no matter what. You can't say that about anyone else."

Before I can shake off my shock at her outburst, she grabs her purse and walks out of the room.

15

The room sits in silence for a few moments after her departure.

Lisa's words echo in my head. *You fucked her over too.*

I could ask myself who she meant, but I already know. Haley. She meant Haley. At least some of my suspicions must be true. Lisa and Haley must have spoken at some point. I'm tired. Tired of wondering what happened to my life. What I did. Lisa says I fucked her and Tyler over. I'm sure she's referring to me cheating. But, how did I fuck Haley over? By going back to Lisa? Did I promise Haley something? Did I wrong her somehow? Maybe by even getting involved with her as a married man? Did I cheat on my wife with a married woman? Did I really do these awful things? I start to wonder about the truth in any of it, yet my underlying feelings for Haley are still there. I'm in love with her, yes. Does that necessarily mean I had an affair? It must mean that. I feel like maybe I'm starting to enter a stage of denial.

If I'm honest with myself, I can't think of any other reason why Haley would risk following us to the science exhibition. Why she'd risk meeting me in that exhibit. Why she'd ask me to find her again. But why run away? I have no real answer about any of this. About anything. It's torturing me, like a splinter stuck somewhere deep in the recesses of my brain that I can't reach to pull out.

The doctor is still standing there. He's picked up my file and is looking through it, or pretending to. In his line of work, I would think he is used to dealing with intense emotional situations like what just played out in front of him, Lisa's outburst has him visibly uncomfortable.

"Doctor?" I say.

"Yes? I'm sorry, Mr. Lewis. Steve. This is certainly a very difficult time. I want you to speak with Dr. Lambert. He'll review everything with you and make sure you understand all the details."

"Doctor?" I say again.

"Yes, Steve?" Lowering the papers in his hands to look at me.

"I have been having mismatched memories. Some which don't make sense at all. I know, I know...Lisa told me. You told her that this can happen. The replacing one memory for another. I'm not sure I buy that. But, doctor, I'm also seeing things. Hearing things. Things that aren't really there. I'm daydreaming and night dreaming and maybe mixing them up. I'm seeing things that don't make sense. Seeing them with my own eyes. I'm not sure what is real and what isn't. I...Maybe I really am losing my mind. I think...I think I am." I blurt out.

"You sound exhausted." Sitting the chart down on the foot of the bed, he just looks at me for a moment, seemingly unsure of how to proceed. "I know it's hard, but this is why I want you to take things slow. An overload of memories or even pushing to try for more memories and not getting them can be detrimental. These things are causing high stress on your body."

"But, the visions. I saw my father yesterday. I mean, I spoke to him. He died years ago, that much I do remember." I say with as much emphasis as I can.

"Thinking that we've seen something or someone that we haven't actually seen. This happens to people every day. People without a condition. It can be caused by lack of sleep, an overactive imagination, lots of things. You aren't going crazy, Steve. You've just got to slow things down." He sounds like a broken record.

"No, Doctor. I had an actual conversation with my dead father. Are you hearing me?" My voice full of frustration from him not seeming to get how crazy this sounds. "An actual conversation. Then...then I passed out, I guess."

He looks stunned again. He takes a deep breath, looks at me, then at my chart, then back at me again, as if some new information will somehow appear on it.

Finally, he says, "Oh." His voice now seems to have lost its energy, his stance on the matter changing."That is certainly concerning."

"Uh, yeah." My sarcasms escaping, now that he's finally coming around to what is completely obvious to me.

"Okay. Let me make sure I'm clear on this, Steve. This does not mean that you're going crazy or dying or anything like that. It does mean that we need to determine what's going on here, medically. I think it goes without saying that I need to keep you here for now. Keep an eye on you. I know you have an upcoming appointment with Dr. Lambert, but with you falling again, he'll want to see you before you leave the hospital. I'll reach out to him today to bring him up to speed. He's typically got a very busy schedule, so I need to see how soon he can come discuss things with you. We need to take time to outline a plan. To..."

"I want to do it."

"Steve, I haven't even reviewed the details with you yet, and I need to discuss things with Dr. Lambert. In light of this new information from you, it could mean a different course of action is in order. Surgery may not even been beneficial in the way that you might be thinking. We..."

"I'll tell you what," I interrupt him again. "I'll meet with him. Once. If you—or if he—do not have a recommendation for a different plan by then, I want to proceed with removing the blockage. This is torture for me, and I'm no longer gaining more old memories like I was at first. If there's even a chance that removing the blockage will change that, I want to take that chance." I'm so emphatic in my reply that he has no choice but to take me seriously.

Another moment of silence between spanning the distance between me and Dr. Bowen before he finally complies, "Okay, Steve. Okay."

16

The day is dragging on. They moved me from the smaller, shared room, to my own room. It's not the one I was in during my first visit here, but it looks very similar, just reversed. I haven't seen the doctor since our conversation about removing the blockage. I've been scanning the television channels pretty much non-stop since I got in here. Lisa called once, apologizing. I told her it wasn't necessary. I told her it was my fault. I apologized for what I must be putting her through. She said she'd come by tonight but I asked her not to. I told her I needed a little space to think about whether or not I want the procedure. Perhaps a bit ironically, she seemed to think the surgery might be a good idea, depending on what the specialist says. I'm a little surprised they are allowing me to even make my own decision about this, considering I am technically brain damaged.

I keep flipping through channels. I still don't recognize most of the shows or actors. I also don't know what time it is. There's a clock in here but the lights are off and the television screen doesn't cast enough light to allow me to see it. I know it's night. I had lunch, then dinner. I feel fine. I'm trying to keep my brain

busy to prevent thoughts or visions. Thoughts about Haley. My
dad. Lisa. Tyler. My condition. The footsteps or ghosts or whatever. I realize I'm thinking about not thinking about these
things, and it's causing me to think about them. Sheesh.

"Mr. Lewis?" The nurse's voice scares me. I didn't hear her
come in.

"Yes?" I sit up in the bed.

"Dr. Lambert is here to see you. He'll only be just another
minute. I wanted to make sure you were awake," she informs me.

It has to be quite late. I suspect he must be here for several
patients and now it's my turn.

"Okay, great. Yes, I'm awake."

She flips on the light, blinding me for a moment. I look over
at the clock. It's 3:20 am. A few moments later, a doctor walks
into the room carrying a large manila folder. He's probably in
his thirties. He's got perfectly parted down the middle, slicked
back black hair and a handlebar mustache. It throws me off for a
moment as I don't think I've ever seen someone—especially
someone so young—with a mustache like that in real life. He
looks like he fell straight out of the nineteen twenties. I'm half
expecting him to say things like "Rahtz!" or "The Bees-Knees!".

"Dr. Lambert, I presume?"

"...and they said you're not acquiring memories anymore." He
jokes, referring to my knowing his name. It's actually a good
point. I am able to make new memories since the initial accident. I hadn't really thought about that until now.

"How are you feeling, Mr. Lewis? May I call you Stephen?" he
asks.

"Totally fine and it's Steve." I clarify.

"Let's just jump right in, man," he exclaims, and I notice he's
got a sort of English or Scottish accent. It reminds me of Sher-
lock Holmes for some reason.

"I'm truly not here to alarm you, and there's no cause for it.

However, swift action is preferred in cases like this, You see, when Dr. Bowen left the message for me, describing your most recent change in status, well...I came to see you as soon as I could," he explains.

"Which change in status is that?" I say. Wondering if he's referring to the blockage or my passing out in the parking lot, or both.

He smiles a big wide smile, his top lip completely hidden by his mustache.

"Why, the visions, of course." Looking at me as if I'd asked the most obvious of questions.

"Dr. Bowen tells me that you've seen strange lights in your house, and heard footsteps. Voices. Yes?" He asks. I nod affirmatively.

"But certainly more notable, you've had a conversation with your deceased father. Correct?" He asks. I nod again.

He grabs the chair by the wall, slings it around and places it beside the bed in an almost exaggerated fashion.

Plopping down in the seat, again a little over animated, he flips open the folder in his hand, revealing a stack of X-ray images. I can see that they are images of a brain. My brain.

"Here's what I think," he says, thumbing through the X-rays and pulling one out for me to see. He holds it up to the light. "See this dark area here?" Pointing to a cloudy grey blob on the image. "The blockage in your brain, which, by the way, I do not think is a cerebral thrombosis." He sees my blank look. "That's a fancy term for blood clot. I don't think that's what it is. In the scans, the mass appears to be more like scar tissue of sorts. He puts the X-ray back in the file and pulls out another one. To me, it looks exactly like the first one. Holding this one up to the light, he points again. "See the light grey shading around the edge here?" I nod, even though I don't see it. "That indicates scar tissue and scar tissue indicates time. Your fall wasn't the cause of this tissue. It's likely been there a while and it's probably some kind of cyst. Don't worry, these types of things are usually benign. What's fascinated me about your case since the beginning is that you have a sort of mix between retrograde amnesia and traumatic amnesia. The first time I've ever seen, or even heard of anything like this. Steve, you may be the first person ever to have this," he states, almost excitedly.

"That sounds either really bad or promising." I point out. "What does it mean?"

"Oh, apologies. Retrograde amnesia describes the symptoms of someone not being able to recall any memories prior to the brain trauma. They can't remember much of anything. Not even from years before it. Memory of language or words are often affected. You have memories of your life up to a certain point. So, you're not a full case for this. On the other hand, post-traumatic amnesia patients typically cannot recall things right before their accident. They remember everything right up to that. But they struggle with obtaining any new memories. You're not a full case for this either." A glimmer in his eye, almost as if my condition has made his day.

"So, this is worse than we originally thought then?" I ask.

"No. Not necessarily. See, the blockage in your brain. Follow along with me here, Steve, I don't want to scare you. I'm going to tell you what we would normally expect to see in these cases, but in this case, we don't. A good thing. A very good thing indeed. See, with blockage like this, blood flow is usually heavily affected. This can cause all kinds of problems like stroke, paralysis, or worse. But you aren't experiencing anything like that. A great sign, I'd say," he expresses, and he's smiling, as if he's just told me that I've won the lottery.

"Okay, so you're saying that I'm lucky it's not worse. But who's to say it won't get worse?" I ask.

"No one is to say that, and it very well could get worse. But I want you to be aware, Steve, the magnitude of effects that you could have experienced from this blockage could have been much worse. You are not experiencing these and for that reason alone, this is good news. But keep in mind, just because you aren't having a stroke, or losing feeling in your limbs does not mean that you aren't experiencing other effects. Things we are not medically used to seeing. Consider that your condition is very rare if not entirely unique. That being so, your symptoms are likely equally as rare, if not unique. There is no scientific or medical reason that these might not include seeing things, hearing things, thinking you are talking to deceased people or people who do not exist." This time he doesn't smile but raises his bushy eyebrows, as if waiting for me to get it and to respond.

"I don't get it. If all of these experiences I have been having, on top of the memory loss, are possible effects of the blockage, then why aren't we discussing removing the blockage as soon as possible?" I ask.

"That is exactly what we are doing, man." He responds patting me on the shoulder, and still smiling.

When I call Lisa and tell her that I've decided to proceed with the surgery, she actually sounds relieved. When I tell her that the doctor has recommended we do it within the next twelve hours, she sounds panicked.

"Please let me come up there," she asks, and the desperation in her voice is heartbreaking. "I know you are going to be okay, but if anything happens to you and I'm not even there... Steve..." and I can tell she's crying.

"Yes. yes. Of course you can come. Lisa, I just didn't want you to think I was crazy, that's all. I wasn't sure myself of that. I'm still not sure. In my mind, the only way I'm going to find out is to proceed with this," I say.

"Okay, I'm on my way. I just need to drop Tyler off at my mom's. Can I bring you something? Anything? Real food?" she asks.

"Thank you, but I'm fine, and they won't let me eat anything now anyway. Not this close to the procedure." I remind her.

"Well, then I'll see you soon," she says.

"Wait," I interrupt. "I know things got heated and we don't

need to revisit all of this right now but I need to know what you meant when you said '*You fucked her over too.*'"

"Steve, I will tell you what I meant." She pauses for a moment, as if she's figuring out how to say this. "I will tell you all the things about this that I know you can't remember. But, please, let's do this first. That's a long conversation and right now we need to focus on you coming through this okay, which you will. But let's focus on you, and after the procedure, I'll explain everything. Okay?"

My curiosity is killing me, but I don't want to fight with her before this procedure, so I agree.

She arrives within the hour. Dr. Bowen comes in shortly after and tells me that he's glad I'm in good hands with Dr. Lambert. He also informs me that I'm scheduled for surgery at 5:00 pm. I get butterflies in my stomach for a moment, but they pass. I know that I can't start living a normal life again until the factors that may be preventing that are removed. The blockage being the main one.

Lisa and I spend the better part of the afternoon watching the television together. I ask how Tyler is doing. She tells me all is well. I doubt that. Annie has apparently been going to the front door and whimpering. Lisa would have me believe that Annie was crying for me. I doubt that too, but even so, it seems ominous. I'm inclined to drift back to what she said before she left. That I fucked everyone over, including *her,* but I push the thought away. I'd like to push all the strange, confusing and mysterious thoughts away until after the surgery. I suppose that I'm expecting all of this to be easier to manage once my brain is fixed. Something I probably shouldn't count on. Around 4:30 pm, two new nurses come in and start getting me prepared for surgery. The butterflies are back in my stomach. The nurses leave the room and come back a few minutes later with a rolling bed. Lining it up beside my bed, they drop the railings, and then half lift, half wiggle me over onto it. I hold up my injured arm to avoid hurting it again. As they're getting me hooked to an IV drip, Lisa leans over and kisses me on the cheek.

"I love you. Please come back to me," she says.

A chill runs across my skin. She said this to me before, except...it wasn't her. It was Haley. I remember. For a moment I start to panic. Maybe I shouldn't do this. Maybe it will cause more problems with my brain. Maybe I'll have a stroke or even die. That memory. Haley. She said those exact words to me. Exactly like that. How would Lisa know this? The nurse starts rolling me out of the room. Lisa follows us out and down the hall. I watch the overhead lights flip by one by one. I'm fading. I don't know what's in the IV, but it works fast. My eyes are closing. I can hear the nurses talking. I hear Dr. Lambert's voice. Lisa's voice. I open my eyes for one more moment. They are rolling me into the operating room. I can't fight the medication. I'm so tired. I must sleep. Closing my eyes again, I hear Haley. "Steve, don't do this. Please wake up."

I'M RUNNING DOWN A TUNNEL, trying to catch up to the person in front of me. Their shape blurry and grey. The floor is slippery and I keep sliding with each step. Reaching out to the walls for support, I notice they are soft and squishy. Looking closer, I see that they are pink and veiny. Like a heart. No, like a brain. I hold onto the walls and walk as fast as I can without falling. The tunnel curving this way and that. Finally, it appears to go in a perfectly straight line. I let go of the walls and break into a full run. I can see the person in front of me. Closer. It's her. She keeps running, yet holds her hand out behind her for me to grab it.

"Please don't let go," she says.

I'm almost to her now. I reach out my hand. The tunnel takes a sharp right turn then straightens again. I slow down to make the turn, slipping a little but not falling. Around the corner, she's further away now. I pick up speed enough to try to catch her. Almost there. Maybe twenty more feet. The path dips down. It's very steep, and at the bottom of the dip, we enter a patch of thick fog. She runs through it, her hands still out behind her.

"Hold onto me. Stay with me," she says, then disappears into the fog. I follow, running as fast as I can. My hands are out in front of me. I enter the fog still running full speed. I can't see where I'm going but I keep running. Suddenly, I hear the rumblings of the tunnel caving in just ahead. Without warning, I run straight into one of the pink, squishy walls. It's soft, like a sponge, preventing me from getting hurt. I push away from the wall, standing back up. Looking around, the fog starts clearing and I can see what I really ran into. It wasn't one of the walls. It's a skin colored boulder made of some sort of fleshy mass. It's lodged in the middle of the tunnel. I can't pass. She is gone. I turn to go back, but the way is unfamiliar. Somehow similar, yet somehow changed.

18

It feels like a hangover. A bad one. My mouth is so dry. My head. Oh, my head hurts. Opening my eyes just a little, I see Lisa. We're back in my hospital room.

"Hi, honey," she says, very softly. Almost a whisper. Walking over to my bed, she rubs my leg through the blanket. "You did great." As if I've just performed some impressive feat.

"Don't try to talk," she instructs. "Everything is fine. I'm so proud of you." Again, with the compliments for my doing nothing.

"My head hurts," I say, and my voice scares me. It sounds far away. Weak. Old.

"Well, you just had brain surgery, silly."

I did. I suddenly feel the butterflies in my stomach again. I survived. I reach up to my head with my right arm. Feeling around, my whole head has a bandage wrapped around it. My fingers run across stubble and the edge of a bald spot near the bandage. They shaved part of my head for the surgery.

"Yes...I did. I...I feel sick," I say.

"The doctor said you might be nauseous. I can ring for the nurse to see about getting you something for that. How's your head? Sore? Is that a silly question?" She smiles a warm, loving smile, making it obvious that she's happy I'm alive yet wary about where we stand.

"I don't feel nauseous, just sick. Like I have a hangover or something. My head? Yeah, I could use something for that. It hurts pretty bad. How do I look?" I say, though I really don't care.

"Pretty rough, to be sure, but things went great, man." Dr. Lambert's voice, interrupting my conversation with Lisa.

Smiling and twirling his mustache, he walks into the room as if it's a day like any other day.

"Splendid, actually. I feel confident that we got all of it. The mass. that is, and we've left only the slightest cosmetic damage to the surrounding area. You'll not see it at all once your hair grows back. It really could not have gone any better."

"So, I'm cured?" I say, knowing that I still don't remember Lisa, or Tyler.

"Well, let's not throw the confetti just yet, man. Yes, I do believe the mass is completely gone. You're cured of the mass, yes, indeed. The lasting effects of the procedure? Well, it may take some time to determine if things have fully returned to normal." He adds, reminding me that the surgery wasn't guaranteed that the puzzles pieces would fit back together.

Still, I have to ask the question. "So, my symptoms, they will eventually go away?"

I look over at Lisa. Her eyes are locked on mine.

"Honey, we didn't expect you to wake up and suddenly remember me," she explains, smiling a gentle smile, and I am relieved.

"In answer to your question, though, yes. You can feel confidant that all of your symptoms will go away, and you'll be back to normal. Tip top." He says, then clicks his tongue in the top of his mouth, making a popping noise.

It suddenly dawns on me that Dr. Lambert is either a genius or a quack. I'm hoping it's the former.

"What happens now?" I ask,

"You rest. Get better. Stronger. We need to monitor you for the next few days at the very least. Expect you'll be going home in a week or so," he smiles.

A week. A week to start getting it together. I hope against hope that I remember everything by then. I can't imagine going back home without remembering Lisa.

Dr. Lambert picks up my chart. He flips through the pages, humming to himself.

"Aside from feeling like you've been on a bender, how do you feel?" he asks.

"Well, that's hard to answer. Beyond the hangover feeling? I can't tell much beyond that right now."

"Fair enough." He drops my chart back into its tray. "Let me, or the nurses, know if and when anything changes, including you feeling better."

"Oh, I will." The doctor gives a wave and walks out, and as the excitement of the conversation fades, I feel the lingering effects of the medication return, pulling me back toward sleep.

"I'm so proud of you for doing this, Steve." Lisa's voice calling to me, and as I turn to talk to her, I feel the sleep taking over.

"Thank...thank you," I say.

"We can talk about what I said before the surgery whenever you want. Now, or maybe after you've had more rest. It's up to you." She smiles and gently strokes my good hand.

I reflect back to before the surgery, and I can't recall exactly what she said. I don't remember anything significant or unsettling.

"What do you mean? What thing that you said?" I ask, fighting the urge to go back to sleep.

I focus to stay awake, noticing a quick flash of a smile on her face.

"Oh, it was really nothing. I'm just being silly." She smiles again, this time it stays on her face for a moment. "Let's focus on moving forward now."

"That sounds perfect," I reply, and it does.

She kisses me on my cheek, then on my lips. I kiss her back, and in the middle of that kiss, sleep finally wins out.

THE NEXT THREE days go by quickly. The pain meds they give me make me incredibly tired and I sleep a lot. It's peaceful and dreamless sleep. I feel physically relaxed, but more surprisingly I also feel mentally relaxed. It seems like a new feeling for me, or at least one I haven't felt in a long time. I feel...peace?

The flowers come again, though not as many this time. Lisa tells me that they are from my friends, some of our employees. There's even one from my mom. I haven't seen Tyler yet since the operation. Lisa feels it's best that I focus on getting better for now. She's stayed by my side except at night, when she's gone back to be with Tyler and her mom. My head feels better, more clear. There is very little pain left. The doctor tells me that all is going well and the scans come back clean — again and again. The days roll by quickly, and with my sleeping so much, they all mesh together.

On the fourth day, I get a memory of Lisa. I think. I'm not sure. I remember her looking at me. I think she was driving. I said something. Maybe it was a surprise. She had a surprised look on her face. I remember those stunning grey-blue eyes. Here, beside me now, I want to tell her, but I decide against it. I don't want to raise her hopes. I know the doctor tells me I will get my memories back. But, what if I don't?

She smiles at me. "Danny called. He's an old friend of yours.

He wanted to know if it would be okay if he comes to see you?" She's strong. So strong. She seems to have handled all of this so well, considering what she's been through with me. She could have just told people to come see me, yet she wants to make sure that I make these decisions for myself. Letting me decide when and how I want to proceed. I feel a surge of something for her. Love?

"Sure, that would be cool." My voice coming out a little shaky, giving away my anxiety about visitors I may or may not remember.

"Really? That's great, Steve." She's holding back her enthusiasm, as if she's afraid to disappoint me. Maybe so she doesn't disappoint herself, too.

Almost two hours later, Danny pokes his head in. The door to my room is wide open, but he knocks on it anyway.

"I'm here to see a guy who claims he can't remember how much money he owes me," he jokes, and I remember him.

"Danny!" I feel my eyes getting misty. "Man, it's so good to see you!" I burst out, not thinking of how it might make Lisa feel.

She smiles, and she does seem genuinely happy for me.

"Steve-o, what the hell? You that hard up for some extra attention?" He jests, walking over to me. He leans down and gives me a hug.

"Danny. Wow. How the hell are you?" I ask.

"I think you did this to get out of helping me with that big project deadline. It worked, so you can go ahead and get better now." He jokes again, half smiling.

Danny Boyle. I've known him for years. I still can't remember how we met, but I expect that will come to me. He has two kids. Girls. Ellen and Elisa. His wife is Elaine. He calls them his threes. A play on the phrase 'three E's'. He loves volleyball. Obsessively so. He's the only person I ever met who follows it on television. He has volleyball 'gear', including black, fingerless volleyball gloves. I used to tease him about it. We meet for wings and beer twice a month at Fannigan's. He sucks at playing darts.

"Wow. So much is coming back to me all at once. It feels...great. I feel like I'm going to be okay," I say, to no one in particular.

"All bullshit aside, man, I'm glad to see you. You need to get better. Keep fighting. We all miss you, bro," Danny says, with an infectious mirth in his voice. So heartfelt that my gut feeling is that I can trust everything about him. The feeling surprises me, at a time when all of my placed trust has been in question up until this point.

"He's been a good sport about everything," Lisa says. "He even pretends to remember the dog." She winks at me.

Danny doesn't say anything or even look over at her, as if he is completely ignoring her. Do they have some kind of conflict? For a moment, I think I might remember that.

"Well, I'll let you two catch up," Lisa says, and it's clear that she's picked up on the vibe from Danny too. She kisses me on the forehead and walks to the door before pausing to add, "I need to run some errands. Go check on Tyler. I'll call you later to see if you want me to bring you dinner. Maybe bring Tyler up here. He misses you." She blows a kiss and walks out before I can respond.

I turn back to Danny. "So...How's Elaine and the kids?" He smiles for a moment and I can tell his answer with that infectious grin. Life is good for him, and he's genuinely happy to see me. I'm happy to see him too.

We talk for the next hour or so, and somewhere during our catching up, I start to fall asleep. It must be the medicine.

"Well, Steve-O, I'll let you rest, man. When you get out of here, we're going for beers. No, I insist. You're buying," he smiles, but I can tell he's holding back tears too.

I hear his fading footsteps as I finally succumb to the desire to sleep. It feels as though I'm only asleep for a moment when I'm awoken by the nurse. The lights in my room are off, and it takes me a moment to see her. My only source of light coming from the wall lamp.

"Mr. Lewis, your wife is on the phone." The nurse, standing over me with the receiver in her hand. "Feel like taking the call?"

"Yeah. Yeah, of course," I say, trying to shake off my nap. I didn't have any dreams this time. "How long was I asleep? It felt like five seconds."

"I'm not sure, but your guest left a little over two hours ago." Handing me the phone, she turns and heads out to the nurse station.

Holding the receiver up to my face, I try to sound as genuine as I can.

"Hey, you." I say. "How's Tyler?"

She acts like she didn't even hear me.

"I'm coming back up there in about an hour. Do you need anything? Food?"

"Nah. I'm good. Looking forward to seeing you," I say, and it's instantly awkward, but I can't put my finger on why that is. It's as if she's upset about something. She had mentioned a conversation we supposedly had before the surgery...referencing something she'd said. I can't recall that conversation, and it makes me wonder if I'm just projecting. Maybe she's just worn out and I'm reading into it. I can't start overthinking things again already.

"Umm... are you still there?" Lisa, still on the phone.

"Oh.. yeah. Yes. I'm sorry. Whatever meds they gave me, they're making me all spaced out," I reply.

"Okay. Well, I'll see ya soon." She hangs up.

I'm left alone for the next hour or so. It gives me time to reflect on my visit with Danny. Seeing him was indescribably good. Like a life raft. One good solid memory of my friend and his family with not one instance of doubt. I know him. I do. He's like the brother I never had. I know his family. I have history with these people. This again makes me wonder why why I still cannot remember my wife and son? The dreaded paranoia starts to sneak in again already. Between that and my overthinking every little thing, I really am going to drive myself crazy. I close my eyes and make a conscious decision to stop this madness and to try and approach things with an open mind. The doctor said he was sure it would all come back to me. After seeing Danny, and remembering him, I do believe that. It's just going to take patience and time. My fear of seeing hallucinations is still there, though not as much. Now that I know the real reasons behind all of them, I feel a little more secure. A little safer.

I start to doze off yet again when Dr. Lambert shows up.

"Steve, you are all cleared for take off, my good man." Twirling his mustache with one hand, he gives me the thumbs up with the other. It seems like a dirty habit for a doctor to keep touching that facial hair, in front of patients, especially.

"All clear?" I say. "How...How can that be? I mean. I still don't...I don't remember everything."

"Well, now, we don't expect you to remember everything just yet. Remember, slow. It will come back this time. Of this, I have no doubt," he exclaims with a quick smile.

"But...doctor...I still don't remember my wife and son. I've got maybe the slightest inkling of a memory of her face, but not really anything concrete."

"Hmm... I must say, I'm not really surprised." I'm on pins and needles waiting for him to finish. "You've been consumed with that fact since the accident, haven't you? I would be. Most any man would be. But, in fact, that concern may be just why it's not coming back yet. You have anxiety about it. You're putting pressure on yourself, and on your brain. Whether you know it or not, you are. She's not helping the situation, man." A knowing look passing over his face, a man-to-man affirmation like he understands the nature of women.

"Wait a minute. She's been the best through all of this. Don't start making her the bad guy..." I start.

"Oh no, man. Not like that at all. I'm simply saying that her desire for you to remember is likely driving you to try even harder. She's been the best. Very loving wife, indeed. But she is human. Her love for you is going to make her sensitive, especially when you seem to have the ability to remember other people...other things...and still not her or your son," he quips, touching his mustache yet again.

"Yeah, well...that makes sense. It doesn't give me any direction here, but it does make sense." I agree, although hesitantly.

"Maybe you should ease off on worrying about which direction you need to take and instead focus on the speed in which you take it. That is, slow. Be patient with yourself. Be patient with her. Be honest. It will come, Steve. It will. The sooner you relax about it, the sooner it will come." He suggests. "You need to tell her that, too."

"Tell who what?" Lisa asks, standing in the doorway.

"Ah, my dear. I was just telling your husband here that he needs to be open about how his mind and body are feeling. No holding back. After all, you are his at-home nurse," he says, with another quick smile. Walking toward the door, he continues. "Mr. Steve is all but ready to walk out of here. We just need to wait for the last few reports to come back. I already know what they are going to say. He's free and clear. But procedure is procedure. Once we get those, we just need to get his final release papers ready and you two can fly," he smiles once more, then bows as if he just finished a play. Spinning around on his heel, he walks out.

"That man is either crazy or an absolute genius," I say, smiling up at my wife.

"Great news that you're ready to go," she replies, and her voice is flat. Like she's acting the part of the devoted wife rather than participating in the reality of this. "Tyler hung back. It's getting a little late and he's tired. But you'll see him tomorrow."

"So, how's your mom?" I ask.

"Do you remember her?" she asks back.

"Well, no. Not really. But I still wondered how she's doing." I want Lisa to understand that I want to remember everything, and that my concern lies not just with myself, but with my family too.

"Why? Why would you wonder how someone is doing who you don't even know? Do you wonder how the patient in the next room is doing?" The irritation in her voice booming, then a flash of agony passes over her face. "Are you concerned for their well being? For their family? Does the thought of what might happen to them if they don't get better keep you up at night? Do you really even give a shit about them?" Tears are welling up in her eyes.

"Who is in the next room?" I ask.

" A person, Steve. There's a human being in the next room. That's about as much as you know about my mom, yet you seem to be concerned about *how she's doing*." She mimics my voice with those last three words, sarcasm lacing her tone.

"Lisa. I just genuinely wanted to know how she is doing." I say, and the road to recovery suddenly seems long again.

For a moment, I think maybe she didn't hear me. She is staring blankly into space, then she sighs and sits down on the chair beside my bed . She's worn out. I can see that she's tired of keeping on her game face. It tells me that it's my turn to be the strong one. Fair enough. I add, "She's been very helpful with Tyler and I'm sure she's been supportive of you, and...I...I just wondered how she is doing."

Her voice softens. She reaches up and gently grabs my hand.

"She's good. A little tired. She won't say it, but it shows. She has always been the strong one."

"Like mother, like daughter." Giving her a knowing glance.

"Ha. I guess." A gentle squeeze of her hand in mine, I see her visibly relax for a brief moment.

"How are you?" I ask, bracing for another harsh response.

"I'm good, Steve. I'm getting you back home. Hopefully for good this time. It's all downstream from here." She says this, and I'm not sure if she means that in a good way or not.

"Yeah. It's all onward and upward from here," I say, trying to verify that we're both looking at this in a positive way, yet neither of our colloquialisms seem to work.

I raise her hand up to my face and kiss it.

"We got this," I say, and maybe it's just that simple.

She smiles. A great big smile this time, and it gives me a feeling of hope.

WE SPEND the next hour watching TV. Mostly quiet. Lisa is exhausted, and I guess I am too. *Wheel of Fortune* is on. I remember it. I remember the host, and I think I've actually seen this exact episode before. It's a repeat, and I remember that much. Things are going to be okay.

"Climb up here," I say, motioning to the bed.

"I'll never fit," she tells me, but she does anyway.

I slide over and she lies down beside me, her shoulder overlapping mine. I'm uncomfortable, but it's worth it. She's asleep before the show is over.

I can't put my arm around her. She's lying on my good one. So I push my head against hers and go to sleep too. We sleep like this for the rest of the night, and it feels right. I wake up in the morning, more rested than I can ever really recall feeling. I feel a renewed sense that everything is okay. Looking over at Lisa, she is turned on her side facing me. She looks peaceful too. I kiss her forehead. She smiles in her sleep, and it makes me happy, confirming for me that I'm ready to go home. The nurse comes in, carrying a stack of papers.

"I thought we were checking out last night?" I ask softly, trying not to wake Lisa.

"You were, but the paperwork took longer than we expected. You're all set now. Just need you to sign a few things and then you can roll. Up and at 'em!" I look down past the foot of the bed and see that they've already put a wheelchair in here. Carefully sitting up without waking Lisa, I take the stack of papers from the nurse and begin flipping through them. Insurance papers, release documents, etc. After what seems like ages, and with a few instructions from the nurse on where to sign and where to initial, I hand the papers back to her.

Sliding back down in the bed, I whisper in Lisa's ear", Lisa, time to go."

She opens her eyes and sits up. "Awesome. Let's get you home, Mr. Lewis." She kisses me on the cheek.

She called me Mr. Lewis. Again, this strikes me with thoughts of my dad.

19

The ride home is pretty quiet. I ask about Annie. I ask about Tyler, then I wonder if she notices that I asked about the dog before our son. If so, she doesn't let on. Apparently all is well. Her mom is dropping him off later today. I scan the buildings and places on the way home. Thinking back to the last time we did this drive home from the hospital, it seems like a dream. Like it wasn't really me. This time, every-thing looks more familiar. More normal, and I feel more at peace, like I'm finally really going home. I look over at Lisa. I'm proud of her. Proud to be with her. She's so strong, and as I'm thinking of that, the little voice of fear in my head starts to chime in, reminding me that I don't really know her. I ignore it. It doesn't matter. I will know her. One way or another, I will. That's all that matters now. My family will be mended. I know this. She catches me looking at her and looks back at me for a moment, then back at the road.

"What are you staring at?" She looks at me, playfully.

"My wife," I say, smiling. "I'm a lucky man, that's for sure."

"Yes, you most certainly are." A little smirk appearing at the corners of her lips.

We pull into the driveway and unload the few items we had in the hospital. My hand feels a little better, but if I try to raise it above my waist, it sends a bolt of pain to my shoulder, reminding me that it's more than just my fingers that were damaged. It's going to be a while before I get this cast off. When we get to the front door, I squat down to see the dog. Lisa opens the door and Annie comes bursting out and straight over to me. She starts licking my hands like crazy.

"Hey, girl! I missed you, too." I say, and she starts wiggling.

"Perfect," Lisa says, reaching behind the door to grab the leash off of a little silver hook. "Here, you guys can catch up while she pees." She tosses me the leash, giggling to herself since I played right into that one. Annie does her business quickly and we head back inside. I head straight for the couch, and...I remember it. The couch. My spot, to the far right, where I can reach the side table. Three remotes are stacked upright in a little wooden tray. I grab the TV remote, turning it on and switching the input to the cable box. I remember all of this. The TV pops on and I turn down the volume. Looking around the room, I remember all of these decorations. The beige and red clay pot in the corner is from Mexico. I was on a cruise there, and this one was hand made and cured in a fire pit. The little wireframe model of the man golfing on the mantle, my mom got me that for my birthday. It has perfectly balanced magnets in it, and works on perpetual motion. If I pull back on the little golf club, he swings back and forth for a while, barely missing the little golf ball with each swing. My memories are coming back again, and with them, a renewed sense of faith. I'm going to keep this to myself this time. I'll wait until I remember Lisa, then tell her.

"Do you have plans today or can we hang out?" I yell toward the kitchen.

"My plans are here with you. That's it."

"Cool. What do you want to do?" I say, thinking of maybe a

movie or something equally as mellow. I'm assuming I'll need to take it easy for a while.

"Well..." She walks out of the kitchen. She's missing all of her clothes and my thoughts of watching a movie diminish, instead locking onto her body as she makes her way across the room. She's fit, and the muscles in her back ripple under her skin as she slowly makes a broad sweep around the living room. Her skin looks smooth and soft. She turns to face me, her breasts full, her tiny nipples hard as a rock. She reaches down with her left hand and pinches her left nipple. Her right hand crawls down her muscular stomach and rests for a moment above the hairless spot between her legs, tempting me. As she approaches me, still sitting on the couch, she smiles and slowly licks her lips. Her performance, and her confidence immediately make me hard. "I was thinking maybe we could get to know each other all over again." She kneels down in front of me.

"You..." I start to say, but she's got my pants unzipped before I can finish. She pulls them down with my underwear, so hard that she almost yanks me off the couch. "Whoa." I say, but I don't resist. Rising up high on her knees, she puts her face to mine and kisses me gently on the lips. Then she leans down, and slides me into her mouth, gently flicking her tongue back and forth. In seconds, I'm throbbing, and I want her. Not her mouth. I try to push up, but I've only got one good hand. My strength fails me and she pushes me back down, keeping me in her mouth. I try once more, this time grabbing her hair with my good hand.

"Oh, you have no patience," she says, pulling her mouth up off of me, her lips wet with saliva. She climbs up slowly and puts one leg on either side of my hips, straddling me. Her skin is hot against mine. Folding her legs back at her knees, I feel her run her warmth across me for the briefest of moments, teasing me again. I pull my bad arm out from between us, placing my good hand behind her neck and pushing her face towards mine. She's strong, and she pushes back against my will. Putting her hands behind her back and onto my knees, she leans backwards and gives me the slightest glimpse at the source of her warmth before quickly leaning back up again.

Both of us silent now, and before I can move, she reaches down between my legs and grabs me tightly. Squeezing me in her hand for a moment, she slowly pushes me up inside of her. When I'm almost all the way in, she stops. We stay still like this for a moment, then she pulls her body up slowly and then back down hard on top of me, sending me deeper inside of her. I recall that neither of us asked the doctor if it was safe to have sex, and attempt to stop her with my good arm. But she brushes it aside and continues. I can't stop her, not just because I only have one good arm, but because I don't want to. I only want her skin and her warmth and her smell and her taste. She pulls herself way up onto her knees, almost to the point of my exiting her, then slams down hard again, pushing me all the way up inside. Deeper still. She's back up on her knees with each reverse thrust, and then down deep onto me again, sending chills all over my body. When I'm buried so deep inside her, she leans in to kiss me, then licks my mouth instead. I'm swimming in her skin and her sweat, her wetness. She's licking my mouth again, and again, like an animal, and I feel her getting wetter. It makes me get harder. Suddenly, she speeds up. Harder and faster. Her perfect heat and tightness gripping onto me with each down stroke. I'm throbbing for release when she starts crying out in pleasure.

"Yes!" She says. "Yes, that's it! That's it!" She grabs the couch behind my head, pulling herself up against me even harder. I try to pull my shirt off with my good hand, but she pushes closer, putting her breasts up into my face. My mouth is all over her skin. I find one of her nipples with my lips and catch it between my teeth. Her smell is all over me. I can think of nothing else.

"Oh, Steve! Oh..." I feel a flood of wetness come over her, dripping down on me. As she comes to a climax, she speeds up, pumping faster than ever. I can't hold out. I feel it building. I'm coming to a peak... and then...as if she can feel me start to explode, she pushes down hard on me once more and stays there. She's tight up against me. Her timing is perfect. I feel myself release into her with such force that it sends me shivering for a moment.

In that exact moment, right when I'm climaxing, she says, "Oh, Steve, I love you."

"I love you, too." I say it before I've even realized what I've said.

"I know you do. I knew it. I could feel it. Through everything. Your broken memory. I knew." She says, and she's kissing me now. All over my face and lips.

A cold fear crawls over me in a wave. Why would I tell her that? Why would I say that now, before I really even remember her.

"We are going to be so happy," she says, standing up pulling me out of her. "We better get cleaned up before Tyler gets here."

She stands, and heads down the hall toward our bedroom. Making my way down the hall, I pass Tyler's open bedroom door. His room is made up nicely. Then I notice that all of his plastic bottle caps are gone. There is no trace of them.

"Hey, where is Tyler's bottle cap collection?" I yell to the bedroom. But Lisa doesn't answer. I hear the shower come on. She probably didn't hear me.

I walk into our room. It is also all cleaned up. Everything in place. I immediately notice that the red mailbox painting is gone too. It never really matched well in here anyway, yet I can't help but find it strange that Tyler's bottle caps and this painting have both been removed since the last time I was home. I head into the bathroom to join Lisa in the shower, but she's done and shuts off the water just as I walk in.

"Hey, where's the..." I start.

She interrupts with, "Babe, I was just thinking. This is truly going to be the start of something wonderful for us. I mean, I feel so happy. Do you know what I mean?"

Still reeling from the fact that I just told her that I love her, I'm determined to not say anything else that I'm not yet sure of. I'm otherwise unsure of what to say and the chasm between her question and my answer is widening. I remember to keep it simple.

"I really think I do. I am happy, too, babe." I kiss her on the forehead.

She smiles and steps out of the shower, grabbing a towel and wrapping it around her.

"Get cleaned up," she calls back to me as she walks out of the bathroom, still dripping water all over the floor.

The hot water feels amazing, and I'm instantly relaxed. With no trash bag covering my cast this time, I almost forget about trying to keep it dry, but remember at the last minute and hold it out awkwardly. What I do forget about is the painting and the bottle caps. After showering, I decide to see if we have any more wine. Walking back down to the kitchen, I see a note in front of the wine rack, as if she knew I'd want wine.

Ran to the market. I'm going to make your favorite tonight. See ya soon. Love you. -L

After a bit of rummaging around in the kitchen, I find the wine and pour a glass. I take a quick walk around the living room. Annie is asleep on her back in the middle of the couch, all four of her legs sticking up into the air. I sit down beside her and rub her belly. She barely moves, apparently too comfortable to be bothered. Surveying the room, I recognize all of this and it feels wonderful. This is my home. My dog. It's little things like this that are going to help me make it through. The memories I do have will lead me to the ones I have yet to find. I know this, and it gives me comfort. I'm no closer to remembering Lisa or Tyler, and I'm starting to realize that I may just have to start over with them. It will come back to me eventually. The doctor is certain of that, though they can't give me any timeline. I assume that it might take days, weeks, or even years. I know in my heart that my best course of action is to play along until I do. It will spare them any more pain. It will help all of us to heal. It will get us past all of this. I will remember her again. I will love her again, and I will tell her again — when I do.

I'm finally truly on my way back to a normal life. Taking a gulp of my wine, I set the glass on the side table. I feel relaxed. Happy. No more strange visions. No more thinking about other people who may or may not have played a part in my past. None of that matters now. From now on, it's about the present and the future. I've only just gotten back from the hospital but I can feel it. I can tell things are different now. Better. I fall asleep on my couch, petting MY dog, in MY living room. Mine.

LISA IS BACK within the hour, but she doesn't have Tyler with her yet. Apparently her mom and Tyler have a playdate today and he'll be dropped off later. After putting food away in the kitchen, Lisa joins me on the couch. It's a tight fit with my bad arm, but it's cozy. Neither of us say anything and it feels nice that we don't need to right now. She kisses me on the cheek, then grabs the remote and starts flipping through channels. I fall back to sleep almost immediately.

. . .

I WAKE to the sound of dishes clanking in the kitchen. Something smells delicious. Lisa is making dinner. That means I've been sleeping all day long. Sitting up on the couch, I see Annie asleep at my feet. She slowly stands up and yawns. It's contagious and I yawn, too. Leaning back into the couch for a moment, I look over to the coat closet. I'm going to look through the photo albums again. Maybe there are other visuals in there that will help my memories come back to me now. I'm opening the closet just as Lisa pops her head in.

"...the door?" Lisa asks. "Steve? Hello? Are you in there? Can you answer the door?"

"Oh, yes. Of course. Sorry," I say.

I hear the tapping on the door, and I know it's Tyler. I can tell by the small sounds of his knocking.

The moment I open the door he throws up his hands and yells, "Surprise!"

"Wow! You surprised me alright!" I say. "Is it my birthday or something?" I ask, teasing him.

"No, silly! But I surprised you!" He runs past me into the kitchen. As I shut the door, I wonder why Lisa's mom didn't come in to say hello, or at least stay long enough to make sure Tyler got inside.

"Is dinner almost ready? I'm pretty sure I died of starvation!" Tyler yells to Lisa.

"Yep. Almost done. Why don't you come help me set the table?" she yells back.

LISA MADE pork chops in applesauce with green beans and slivered almonds. Apparently this is my favorite meal. A memory I don't have back yet. Regardless, dinner is wonderfully noisy, with Tyler exclaiming every sentence. He's a cute kid. Lisa is so patient with him, reminding him not to interrupt, to wait his turn, to chew with his mouth closed. I feel like they are both genuinely excited to have me home and it warms my heart. This is my family, and for a moment, the fear and anxiety of not remembering them is gone. They love me. They miss me. They need me. I promise myself I won't get emotional yet again, smiling at each of their stories. Lisa has been running things at work even through my second episode. Tyler's new favorite color is red, and he is deathly afraid of clowns (something he's apparently told me many times before). Annie caught a baby squirrel a few weeks ago. Tyler is convinced she was trying to save it but it was too late. Lisa adds to this theory, then winks at me across the table, saving Tyler from the truth about dogs and squirrels for now. I barely get more in than an, "Oh, wow, really?" or "I see" before dinner is over and Lisa starts cleaning up. Tyler joins in and I assume that's my queue to get out of the dinning room. Lisa walks over and gives me a quick kiss on the cheek.

"Why don't you take Annie out then hit the couch and take it easy, old man." Her smile is genuine and mine is too.

"Old? Oh, okay, I see how it is." I smile at her and head for the back yard with Annie right on my heels. The evening air is clean and crisp, adding to my sense of peace, as if to remind me that I'm finally on my way to getting my life back. Annie finishes quickly and waits outside the door.

"You're such a house dog, girl!" I tell her.

Back inside, I head for the couch. Annie beats me to it and I have to scoot her over to make room to sit. I hear Lisa calling to Tyler to get ready for a bath. She puts so much work into all of this. Dinner, Tyler, our company. My arm and hand hurt a little, but not bad. Otherwise, I feel fine. For the first time in...in as long as I can remember. I do. I feel fine, even good. Almost great. With that though in my mind, I decide that there's no use in waiting any longer to fully invest in my life, even if I can't recall most of it. I'm going to work tomorrow. Even if just to check and see if it brings back any memories. If it doesn't, I'll be fine. I'll relearn the business if I have to. From here on, no looking back. Deciding that I should get as much rest as possible for my first day back, I retire, telling them both goodnight along the way. I can't get to sleep right away, maybe because I slept all day. Just as I'm finally falling asleep, Lisa joins me.

"Hey, you. Still awake?"

"Yeah. Is it possible to overdose on sleep?" I joke.

"Not for an old man like you." She jokes back.

I sit up a bit, shaking off the sleepiness I was starting to feel. "Hey...I was thinking, I know I just got back home, and I need to take it easy and all, but I really want to go to work. Even if just for a day," I say, expecting her resistance.

"No way, babe. You need to rest more first." She replies. "I understand you're getting stir crazy, and maybe we can plan another outing this weekend. Something more mellow and closer to home. But work already? That's just too soon."

I take a little breath, deciding on how best to ease her mind. "Look, I know it's too soon. I do. I get that, really. I'm not talking about going back full time yet. I just want to see where I work. See the people I work with. Maybe it'll jog some memories. Maybe it won't, but regardless, it's a big part of my life...of our lives together. I need this. I really do. I promise not to push it. I'll just go by there for like an hour or so." I say, looking at her earnestly. Sincerely.

"Okay. Your call." She tells me. "But for the record, I protest this." Giving me another kiss on my forehead, she continues. "I'll drive you in the morning, but you have to promise me. Promise me. If you feel anything less than good, you'll call me immediately to come get you."

"Scout's honor," I say, holding up two fingers.

"Okay then, get some sleep, Mr. Overachiever." She kisses me on the lips this time.

I go to sleep with butterflies in my stomach. I'm actually excited to see what my company is like. Excited...and a little scared.

20

The night seems short, yet we actually sleep in. We aren't up and getting ready until past ten in the morning. I slept great. Dreamless, peaceful sleep. Breakfast is coffee and quick toast and we're loading up in my truck soon after.

"Do I need to bring anything?" I ask her.

"Just your lunchbox, your backpack, paper and pencils." She teases, although she did pack my lunch.

"Okay, Mom." I tease back.

The drive to work is remarkably short. Less than fifteen minutes by my count. It makes me wonder if we bought the house because it was so close to the office, or if we rented the office because it's so close to the house. Regardless, being in such close proximity is nice. "The shop" as she calls it, is a single-story, light brown building with a small parking lot, sitting just off the main road. It's tucked in between a fifties-style diner and a boutique pet store. Lisa turns off the ignition and starts unloading with Tyler. I work my way out of the passenger seat and walk around the truck to meet her.

"Hey...I can do this, babe," I say.

"I know you can. I just figured I'd walk you around. Get you reacquainted with things." She smiles.

"I appreciate that. I really do. But, I want to do this on my own. To face the challenge. I think I need to," I say, glancing at the front door.

She reaches out, gently grabbing my chin between her index finger and thumb, turning my face to meet hers.

"I understand." Her eyes alit with an understanding. "You've got this."

She smiles again, and I feel a spark inside me light up for her. I can see how I loved this woman. I can see how I'll be able to again.

"Thank you," I say, giving her a quick kiss.

I grab my lunch as they load back up in the truck.

"Call if you need me, even if it's just to cut out early!" She calls from the window as they pull away. I give a thumbs up and turn toward the office building. There's no official sign by the road, but a faded white van sits in the parking lot with the words 'Living Color Painting' running along its side, with the office phone number listed under it. It's a clever company name, but it doesn't bring any memories back to me. There's a single glass door under a green awning with white trim. A long, black, rubber mat lays on the pavement in front of it. It looks like one of those mats that triggered automatic doors in storefronts back in the eighties, but the door has a sign on it that says 'Pull'. There's a stenciled painting of the company name on the door. I take a deep breath and walk toward it, noticing that the sky is suddenly overcast. A fine misty rain starts just as I open the door. I hear a little chime and see a tiny little gold bell hanging by a bright red ribbon in the door spring.

"Well, hello, Steve!" The voice startles me and I jump.

A plump little woman with a buzz cut sits behind a high desk. It looks like a checkout counter that's been converted into a reception desk. The whole interior of the building looks like it was originally designed as a sort of showroom, but it's now being used as a storage room for paint and painting supplies. A wide open space with an open ceiling and a set of small rooms off to one side.

Looking back to the woman, I see she's still staring at me.

"Um..hi. How are you?" I ask her.

"I'm great, boss. Great to see you. We'd heard you might not be here for a while."

"Well, I've been spending so much time lying down. I figured it's time to get back on my feet." Realizing how familiar that sounds, I give this stranger a small smile. Her voice is so distinct. It's raspy, yet high pitched and it seems so familiar to me.

"True enough. We heard you've got amnesia. That so?" she asks, bluntly.

"I can't recall everything no, but I'm getting there. Little by little." Her direct question surprises me a little. I assume maybe this woman has worked for me for a while and perhaps she knows me pretty well, but not remembering her, I'm a little put off by her bluntness .

"Well, welcome back. Let me know if there's anything I can do for you. Lisa has been here quite a bit, but your office is pretty much just like you left it." She tells me.

"Thank you...umm..." I stall, scanning the room for anything familiar. I find nothing that is.

"Wow. That's amazing." She expresses, openly smiling. "You don't remember me. I'm sorry, Steve, but it's just kind of weird. Like, we have talked almost every day for the past two years. It's just crazy, that's all. I mean, I hope you're okay. I really do. But it's just so strange." She's still smiling, still not telling me her name.

"I know. It's strange to me too. It feels like I'm being rude, but I can't help it. I'm getting better, but I'm not quite there yet."

"Well, I'm not offended, Steve. Not one bit. Want me to show you to your office?"

"No. I mean, thanks, but...maybe you can just point?" I ask.

"That way." She points down the hall and off to the left. "Straight back. The hall pretty much dead ends into your office."

"Great. Thank you." I say, walking towards the hall. "I hate to ask, but...what's your name?"

"Oh, wow. That's right. So weird. I'm sorry. I'm June. June Goodall. I'm your receptionist, accountant, and administrative assistant. I pretty much do everything but paint."

"Well, it's nice to meet you again, June Goodall. I'll be in my office for a little while."

I take a few moments to walk out to the shelves of paint and supplies. Although I'm kind of impressed that we have our own company, 'the shop' isn't so impressive. It's basically just a warehouse. Hundreds of paint cans line the shelves in various sizes. There are three big machines in the far corner. I think they are paint mixers. Poles, brushes, and sprayers adorn a section of the east wall, in between more shelves. The whole place smells like lumber and paint. There's not much else to see here, and none of this brings back any memories for me.

Walking back past June's desk, I ask, "June, sorry to interrupt again, but where is everyone?"

"Out painting, boss. Where else?" she informs me, looking at me as if I've just asked a really dumb question. I guess I have.

"Of course." I laugh at myself. "How many trucks do we have?"

"Zero trucks, Steve. But we do have four vans. One of them is damn near brand new." Saying proudly, as if it's her personal vehicle.

"Ahh, okay. Got it. Thanks, June. I think I remember that," I say. I really don't remember that at all, but as soon as I walk into my office, I do remember it. The walls are painted a dull grayish color. It's well lit in here, but for some reason, there is still a desk lamp on. I put my lunch down on the side table and walk over to my desk. It's really two desks. One of them is a flat, polished oak desk. The other desk, set up next to the first one, is an angled desk with a crossbar in the middle. The crossbar rides along tiny metal cables on either side of the top of the desk. It's a drafting table. I pull up the black leather office chair and sit, taking a closer a look at things. The flat desk has a black plastic office phone sitting on it, the red message light blinking away. Surprisingly, there's no computer here. Maybe I have a laptop at home somewhere. A few envelopes lay in a wire-framed in-box. They've all been cut open with a knife or a letter opener. I pick through a couple of them. Invoicing and receipts for checks from various painting jobs. It looks like we do both commercial and residential work. None of the paperwork strikes a memory for me. Looking up, I see a cork board on the wall. A few pictures of various buildings are pinned to it. I'm assuming these are buildings we've painted. There's also a drawing pinned to the board with one of those old-school flat metal thumbtacks. I reach out to pull it down when my desk phone rings. The display across the phone reads 'XFER FROM RECPTION'. I lean out enough to look down the hall. I can see June at her desk from here. She looks up and sees me looking at her.

"Oh, shit. I'm sorry. I just sent that one to you. Old habit. That's a call from Mr. Ellison. He owns a strip mall that we're painting. You can let it roll to voicemail. I won't send you anymore calls for now." She tells me, looking apologetic.

"No problem. Yeah, I think I will let it go to voicemail," I say. I don't remember a Mr. Ellison, or a strip mall project. Best to let Lisa handle this type of stuff for now, at least until she brings me up to speed.

Reaching back up, I pull the drawing down off the cork board. It's done in pencil, but it looks like it was drawn with drafting tools. The lines are perfectly straight. It's a floor plan of a house. My house. All of the electrical systems are drawn in. Outlets, panels, wiring, switches, etc. I'm guessing that maybe I designed our house's electrical systems. Looks like I didn't completely let go of my dream of becoming an engineer. But, why would I decide to get into a painting business? What a strange choice. My desk phone rings again. Apparently, we are busy. I look at the display on the phone again. It reads 'DIRECT FRM BCKLINE'. Leaning out again, I see June at her desk. She's turned away from me, with a stack of papers in one hand and pencil in the other. I look back to the phone. Who's calling me directly through a backline? A hint of paranoia hits me for just a brief moment before I realize it's probably Lisa. It dawns on me that I don't have a mobile phone, which seems really odd. I decide to ask her about that. I pick up the phone.

"Hello, this is Steve Lewis," I say.

There's nothing on the other end. Just silence.

"Hello? This is Steve. Is anyone there?"

More silence, but now I hear someone breathing.

"I can hear you breathing. Hello?"

Nothing.

"Okay, hanging up now." I tell this silent stranger.

"Steve..." A voice on the other end. I feel like I know that voice. A woman.

"Steve...I keep hoping against hope that you'll come back to me. I try to stay positive, babe. I try so hard to, but it's getting harder and I'm losing faith." She tells me.

Her voice floods my brain and it comes back to me. The voices. The footsteps. My dad. The note on my bandage. Her perfume. The science exhibit. All of the memories of her I'd gained since the accident. The visions I've seen. I remember her name. It's Haley.

I'm afraid June is going to hear me but more afraid to get up and shut the door. I don't want Haley to hang up. My heart is in my throat as emotions that I did not know existed a few moments ago flood through me. I love this woman.

Doing my best to whisper, I ask, "Haley, how do I know you? Did we have an affair? Are you still married? Please don't hang up. I need to talk to you. My memory is all messed up since the accident. I want to remember. Help me."

"Listen, Steve, it's getting late and I need to run home..." Her voice sounds so tired.

I look at my watch. It's twelve minutes past noon. Late? My watch. It reminds me of something...but what?

"Why are you calling me if you can't talk? I need to know what happened. I need to know what's going on between us," I say.

"I'll be back early tomorrow morning. Stay strong." She says these words, but I have no idea what she's talking about.

"Be back where?" I ask. "Where are you going? Where are you know? I need to meet with you, please."

"I... I love you, Steve." Her voice cracks at the end, and I can tell she's about to cry.

"I love you too," I say, and although this woman is now a stranger to me, I know that I do.

She doesn't hang up but I here footsteps through the receiver, getting more and more faint, as if she accidentally left the phone off the hook. Did she forget to hang up? Looking around my office again, something nagging at me. It's now silent on the phone. Why is Haley calling to tell me she has to go? How is it late when it's morning? Is she in a different time zone? I look at my watch again, then back around the room. What is it? A memory? So close. Then, it comes to me. Another memory I've already had since the accident but forgotten again since the surgery. My office. This is my office, but it's all wrong. It's supposed to be in a big building, on the seventh floor. It's in a bigger office, not some painting warehouse. There was a window in my office but it's not here. I remember looking at my watch, then out the window. She was there, in my memory. Haley was there, outside the window. A bigger question clouds my thoughts. How, since the surgery, did I forget about this again? What else have I forgotten since then? Did the surgery actually cause more memory loss? I'm starting to get used to having lots of questions and very few answers.

I spend the next hour looking around my office for clues, but find nothing that helps. Although Haley never hung up, she was no longer there. I listened for a while, but only ever heard other faint voices occasionally talking, as if she was in a public place when she called. I eventually hang up the phone. Giving up on finding anything helpful in my office, I decide to call Lisa to come get me. It takes her less than five minutes to get here and that makes me wonder if she's been parked somewhere, just waiting for my call.

June calls over my phone's speaker, "Boss, I see Lisa just pulled up out font. I'm assuming she's here to get you. Really putting in the overtime today, huh?"

"Thanks, June. I'm coming out." I answer into the speaker-phone, realizing I could have just shouted down the hall.

As I'm making my way toward June's desk, I realize I forgot my lunch. Just as I step back into my office to grab it, my phone rings again. 'DIRECT FRM BCKLINE' comes up on the display again and my heart stops. Lisa is just outside the building in the truck. I kick my door closed and grab the phone.

"Hey, don't hang up!" I say, all at once.

"Why would I hang up? I'm here. You ready, babe?" Lisa's voice.

I pause a few seconds before I say, "Hi. Yes, I was just grabbing my lunch. I never got a chance to eat it yet." Hoping my voice doesn't sound stunned.

After I grab my lunch and walk for the door, June calls out.

"I was just hackin' on you about working late. Hope you feel better real soon. We all miss you, boss."

"Thanks, June. I hope I'm all better soon, too," I say, walking outside.

Climbing back into the truck, Lisa immediately asks.

"Why'd you tell me not to hang up?"

"Oh, I was just walking back into my office from talking to June and I wanted to make sure you stayed on for a minute while I put you on hold to grab my lunch," I say, knowing it makes no sense.

"Ummm...Okay? How was your day, or...your couple of hours?" she asks.

"It was fine, I guess. I don't think I'm ready just yet. We had a client call who I don't remember. I guess I don't really see myself adding much value to the company if I can't remember any of our clients." I take a breath.

"Well, don't rush it, babe. It'll all come back you." She reminds me, and that last part echoes over and over in my head.

I need it all to come back to me. This woman, these memories from after the accident I'm getting back. The science exhibit, I remember it. I remember seeing Haley, and running after her. I remember falling again. Why have I forgotten this?

I'm lost in all of these thoughts all the way home before I notice that both Lisa and Tyler have been dead silent all the way back here. Not a peep from either of them.

When we get home, Annie seems to be the only one that's happy. Tyler remains strangely silent, and Lisa just seems generally irritated. Perhaps this is simply the way things are in married life with a child, I tell myself. But the reality is, we've all been through a lot and I know it's going to take some time. I'm not the only one who needs to recover. Lisa heads down the hall to put Tyler down for his nap, and I take the opportunity to tell her I'm going to take one too. I'm back in my bedroom and in bed before she's done with him. I hear her walking down the hall to me, here in our room, and I fake being asleep. She opens the door and then closes it back, so it takes me a few minutes to realize she's not in here.

From out in the living room, I hear her calling Annie.

"Come on, girl! You need to go outside?"

I hear her fumbling with the leash, then I hear a door shut. Quickly, yet as quietly as I can, I get out of bed and peep through the window blinds. Lisa is walking down the sidewalk with Annie on her leash. It looks like they're going for a walk. Lying back down in the bed, my thoughts again move toward finding Haley. I know that it's just not right, but the feeling that there are things I still don't know, things that Lisa is hell bent on hiding from me, makes me want to know even more. If I cheated on her and fell in love with my mistress, then I need to know that. I'll do what's right, I tell myself. I'll stay with Lisa and I'll never talk to Haley again. The thought hurts me worse than anything I can recall, but I will. Regardless, I first need to know exactly what happened. I cannot live the rest of my life wondering. Thoughts start racing through my mind about how I can meet Haley again in person to find out the truth. She's obviously following me or she'd never know I was at the science center, or my office. That means she's either in the neighborhood, or she sits outside of it and waits for me to leave. The second part of that theory seems very unlikely, so I'm left to believe that she lives in the neighborhood. That seems like the only logical explanation. I start dissecting that thought when I notice the red mailbox painting hanging on the wall again. What the hell? I remember this being here, then gone. Now it's back? I start to get up to go over to it when I hear several sets of footsteps in the hall, moving quickly and getting closer to my door. These are adult footsteps; I can tell by the sounds.

I start to panic, holding my breath in anticipation of my bedroom door opening. Nothing, the footsteps seem to walk right past. Then, I hear them coming back. How could other people be in the house? Unless...unless they were already in here before we got home. Is it Haley? Did Lisa sneak back in? I see the doorknob start turning and fear takes over.

"Who's there?" I want to shout, but I find my voice is frozen and nothing comes out.

The door opens, but no one is there. I hear the footsteps entering my room. They come right up beside me. Then, I feel it on my wrist. Something soft and warm. It takes me a minute to realize it's a hand holding firmly onto my wrist. I try to move, but

I can't. I try with all my might to speak. I feel my lips forming the words.

"Ww..." It's all I can get out.

"Steve!" A voice yells, right beside me.

Several sets of footsteps all around me. Then, a bright light in my right eye. It's blinding, yet I can't look away. A second later, it stops, leaving me temporarily unable to see much out of that eye. The light comes on in my left eye and is gone again a moment later. My heart is pounding out of my chest but I can't move. I'm paralyzed, not just with fear, but literally. I cannot move. I'm stuck lying here.

Then, just like that, it's all gone. I test my voice.

"Hello?" I say into the empty room.

I scan the room, oblivious to anything but finding out what that was. Opening the bedroom door, I find the hall empty. No sign of anyone. I methodically check all the doors in the house. They are all locked up tight. I decide to do a room-by-room check of the windows. All of them are locked as well. The only room I haven't checked is Tyler's because he's sleeping. For a moment, I have a flashing thought of an intruder hiding in his room, having come in through his unlocked window. I decide to risk waking him and check his windows too. Slowly and carefully, I reach for the knob on his bedroom door. My hand instinctively pulls back when I feel the cold metal. I grab it again, gently, and push the door in. Peering into his room, I see him in his bed, under a pile of blankets. He is sleeping peacefully. A good sign. As I tiptoe in, trying not to wake him, a wave of frigid air hits me. It's freezing in here. As silently as possible, and not at risk of waking him, I walk past his bed. I don't want to alarm him, and I quickly decide that, if he wakes up, I'll tell him that I was just checking on him. Pausing for a moment, I look down at him again, still in slumber. The odds of someone coming in through the window and not waking him are pretty slim. His room is dead silent. Gently reaching in past the curtains to check the locks, I notice that the window is covered in condensation. The temperature in this room can't be good for him, and I make a mental note to ask Lisa if it's always so cold in here. I check the lock on the window and find it securely fastened, not surprisingly. There is no sign of an intruder, further confusing me of how someone could have gotten into the house. Turning back around to leave the room, I see Tyler standing right next to me. His face pale. His eyes rolled back in his head, exposing their whites. His mouth is wide open in a silent scream. He has his right arm raised, pointing his index finger right in my face.

I cry out, falling backwards into the wall. "Ahhh!!"

In the blink of an eye, he snaps his mouth and eyes shut, like a machine. Then he turns, gets back into bed, and starts gently snoring. I regain myself, my heart slamming like a jackhammer. I approach the bed reaching out to gently shake him. His skin is cold and dry.

"Tyler. Tyler. Son... wake up, buddy."

I shake him harder and raise my voice. "Tyler. Tyler! Hey! It's Dad! Wake up!"

He doesn't stop snoring.

I shake him violently. "Tyler! Tyler! Hey!! Wake up!'"

Continuing to snore, he doesn't otherwise move an inch. I leave his room and walk down to the kitchen, looking for Lisa, half expecting more footsteps, voices, or lights.

Pacing the hall and the living room, I try to recall the exact sequence of events with the footsteps. They came up to the door, then past. Then they came in the room. Why couldn't I see anyone? Is this house haunted? A notion I've never believed in. What the hell was Tyler doing, and why can't I wake him now? Walking back through the living room, I notice the cardboard box in the floor, the corner, behind the sofa chair. The box that

Lisa brought back from the hospital the first time. It has the cards and vases from the flowers people sent. Using my good hand, I drag it out away from the wall and open it. Several cards are strewn about in the box, along with a few colored vases and remnants of dried up flowers. I grab a few cards out at a time, stacking them on the floor. Once I've got them all out, I sit up in the sofa chair and go through them.

The first one has a cartoon dog on the front with a thermometer sticking out of his mouth and a caption that reads, "Hoping you rest and heal soon knowing you are in our thoughts." I open the card...and it's blank inside. No more print and no one signed it. Odd, perhaps a mistake. Someone forgot to write in it. I flip to the next card. A daisy and the caption, "Hoping you get well soon..." I open the card and inside it's printed "...and prayers for a speedy recovery." Again, there's no signature. It's blank. Strange. I open the next card and skip past looking at the outside to see who signed it. It's the same as the first two in that there's no signature. It's blank. The next card is the same, and the next one. I frantically start going through the remaining cards. All of them are blank. Then it dawns on me, no one actually sent me any of these cards. They are all from Lisa.

I'M SITTING HERE, in shock. What the hell is going on? Lisa staged the flowers. She wanted me to think I had people wanting me to get better and thinking about me, but why? She wanted me to think people were aware of my accident. I get on my knees in the floor to see if there are any other clues in the box, when I hear Lisa outside.

"Come on, girl. Time to go in." I hear Lisa say to Annie, just outside the front door.

Quickly throwing all the cards back in the box, I slide it back to the corner. Just as Lisa is opening the front door, I stand, spin and look out the back window of the house.

"Hey, you. What are you doing?" She questions.

As casually as I can manage, I turn from the window.

"I was actually looking for you. I checked on Tyler. I think he might me sick or something. He was out of bed for a minute, acting strange, then went right back to bed and fell asleep. I can't wake him now."

"Oh, babe, I guess I forget that you don't yet remember some things." She looks surprisingly calm. "Tyler sleepwalks sometimes and he's hard to wake up right after." She acts as if it's the most common thing ever.

I can't describe the terrifying look of horror on his face, so I don't try to.

"Are you sure?" I ask, my voice shaking. She doesn't seem to notice. "He's been looking so pale lately, like he might really be sick."

"I'll check on him, but I really am sure he's okay. He gets a little bit like that sometimes, but he's fine." She's not even the slightest bit worried.

She leans down and takes off Annie's collar, then walks into the kitchen.

"Hey, you need to get ready before too long."

"Ready? Ready for what?" I ask.

"Just for dinner," she replies.

"Are we going somewhere?" I ask.

"Nope. But get showered and ready anyway." She says with a wink.

I'm so tempted to ask about the cards, but I'm afraid if I expose her lies openly, she'll just add more lies to cover them. No, I've got to figure this out on my own. The footsteps and the invisible hand touching mine minimize the blank cards, and the incident with Tyler, making me again wonder if I am going crazy.

"Okay, I'll go get ready now," I say, and head back for the bedroom.

I take a long, hot shower, lost in thought about the footsteps, the hand, the voice, the cards, all of it. Even if I do have some sort of brain damage that's causing hallucinations, I know the cards were real. I'm sure of it. I'm starting to get the sense that she's managing my every move to see if I'm taking the bait, whatever that is. Maybe even taking advantage of my brain damage to trick me. By the time I get out of the shower and back in the bedroom, I notice that Lisa has been in here. The bed is made, and the mailbox picture is gone again. Why would she keep adding and removing a picture? Is it like some kind of mind game to test my memory skills?

I decide to go ahead and get dressed and ready for this dinner that she's so mysterious about. Not having any idea why I'm supposed to get dressed for dinner, I find a light blue, pull-over collared shirt and a pair of casual, beige slacks. I even put on a pair of loafers, suddenly feeling a little overdressed for dinner at home. As I'm coming down the hall, I hear Tyler stirring in his room.

"Are you going to be my daddy?" I think I hear him say through the closed door. A chill runs over my skin again. Half afraid of another terrifying encounter with him, I remind myself that this is my son. I turn back and go to his room, putting my ear against the door. Listening for a few moments, I hear nothing and decide to check on him. Quickly opening the door this time, as a sort of measure against getting startled again, the coldness of the door handle and his room hit me at once. It's no wonder he's always bundled up under the covers. Walking over to him, he is again dead asleep. I look at his face, trying not to focus on the sleepwalking event that scared me so. Sitting down on the edge of his bed, I study his face, trying so hard to remember him. I'm sure I heard him incorrectly through the door. My mind must be playing tricks on me. One of his hands is hanging out of the covers, and I hold it with my own for a moment, wishing for even the slightest memory of him. Anything to help bridge the gap between us. His skin is cold, and I again tell myself to ask Lisa about the temperature in here. I gently pull his hair back out of his face. He looks so unhealthy, like all of this has taken it's toll on him too. His skin is so pale. His eyes look sunken, like he's not had enough sleep. His lips almost have a bluish tint. He looks...he looks dead. A stabbing fear hits me in the chest. I put my hand in front of his lips to see if I can feel him breathing. Just as I feel myself starting to panic, he stirs again and rolls over, facing the wall. I take a deep breath, and realize how on edge I am as a result of this day. Taking another deep breath, I lean down and kiss him on the cheek.

"It's going to be okay, son," I whisper, knowing he can't hear me.

I stand as quietly as possible and walk over to his door. Just as I start to close it behind me, I notice them. His entire bottle cap collection is back.

I'm standing here in the hallway outside of Tyler's room, trying to calm down before going out into the kitchen to confront Lisa. The magically disappearing and reappearing picture and bottle cap collection have me wondering if the voices and the footsteps are also Lisa's doing. Some sort of psychological experiment on me to see what I can remember, or maybe just to mess with me as a form of payback for my infidelity. This, of course, makes no sense at all since I could not see who or what was touching me, but I'm grasping for straws at this point. The idea creeping in that my brain is so damaged that I may need to spend the rest of my life in some sort of facility, for the safety of others and of myself. I think maybe I'm truly going mad. It's with these thoughts of madness that I go down to the kitchen to greet Lisa and pretend that everything is completely normal.

"Hey, you. Anything I can help with?' I ask, feeling almost as if I must be joking at this point.

Lisa has several pots on the stove, and she's cutting up tomatoes and onions.

"Nope, I've got this." Smiling, she adds, "Why don't you get a drink and just chill on the couch? You should milk the brain damage thing for all it's worth, you know? Once you get better, it's back to the grind."

I can't help but notice that she's calling it brain damage just as I'm thinking of it that way. Coincidence? I doubt it, although that would mean she can read my thoughts. Maybe she wants me to drink so it's easier to trick me? Deep down, I know that even my entertaining the notion of her being able to read my mind is surely another sign of madness.

"I think I'm going to chill on the drinking for now." I look at her to gauge her reaction. "I think maybe too much wine along with my meds isn't good for me."

I notice her eyes dart sideways over to me the moment I suggest I'm not getting a drink.

"Oh...okay, that makes sense, I suppose," she says. "Well, if you need anything, just let me know."

"I will and thanks," I say, and as casual as I'm trying to be, I can't bring myself to walk over and touch her or kiss her. Her deceptions are front and center in my thoughts, and I'm only so good of an actor.

I'm on the couch for five minutes or less before Tyler comes tearing down the hallway. Surprising, considering how he seemed out cold just a few minutes ago. Then, I think of his silent scream trick and how he was able to get up and be standing beside me as quickly and quietly as a ninja.

"Mom. Is dinner ready? Can we eat now? I'm so hungry. So hungry." He repeats.

I lean back far enough to get a view of him standing in the kitchen next to Lisa. He looks ill. She turns and looks down at him, and I see a look of sadness on her face. There's no mistaking it. "It's ready, but we're waiting a little while longer, remember?" She bends over, then whispers something in his ear.

"Oh. Okay. Yes, we need to wait for Daddy's surprise," he says, and his voice seems different, almost as if he's reading.

"Okay, what's the big surprise?" I ask, getting up off the couch and walking back into the kitchen.

"We can't tell you because it's a surprise," Tyler says, smiling up at me. A strange look in his eyes.

"Fair enough." I decide to play along. "But now I'm super excited!"

What I don't say is that I could I do with anything other than a surprise right now. I don't know what's real and what's not at this point, but I need time to think. Time to dissect all of this. I'm paranoid of everything my wife does or says, and I'm starting to feel like my son needs some sort of medical attention. The next thirty minutes or so go by painfully slow. I find myself pacing around the living room. Lisa is obviously delaying dinner for something. Just as I'm wondering what the hell that could be, the doorbell rings.

"Do you mind getting the door?" Lisa calls from the kitchen.

"Sure. I've got it." I yell back towards the kitchen, walking to the front door.

I open the door and see my mom staring me in the face. Through her pre-canned smile, she says,

"Oh, son. It's so good to see you."

After staring at her in shock for a moment, and then helping her in with her things, my mom heads into the kitchen to see Lisa and Tyler. She brought a large suitcase with her. I struggle getting it into the living room with my one good arm. My first thought is that she's planning on staying for a while. This scares me as much as the visions and my broken memory. I don't think I can handle her being here long, especially as I'm trying to recover and figure things out.

"Hi, Mom! Thank you so much for coming. How was your trip?" Lisa asks, with a resounding tone of fake cheerfulness. She half-hugs, half-shakes my mom's hands.

Mom smiles again, but doesn't answer and instead walks straight over to Tyler. As soon as she sits down at the table, he climbs up next to her.

"Lisa, can you help me with this?" I say, walking back out to the living room.

"With what?" She asks, pulling off her oven mitts and walking out behind me.

As soon as we're in the living room and out of sight from my mom, I turn to her and whisper.

"Please don't take this the wrong way but you must know that my mom and I don't have a very good relationship. I sincerely appreciate the surprise, but please tell me she's not staying here." I'm unable to hide the desperation in my voice

"You never told me that you guys don't have a good relationship. Not even once. I was only trying to help. I figured she'd be a nice familiar face. You haven't seen her in a while, and you could stand to catch up, even aside from your accident." I suddenly see a deep anger in her eyes that I've not seen before. Before I can process it, it's gone and she's looking at me as if I've hurt her. Sadness sits on her face for a moment.

"It's not your fault. I guess I've not been as open about my relationship with her as I should have been. It'll be fine. Thank you trying to help me." I tell her. "But, is she planning on staying here?"

"Yes, but just for the night. It's a two-hour bus ride each way for her. That probably doesn't seem like much, but with her hip, it takes a lot out of her." Her attempt to guilt me into being okay with it actually works, especially since it is only one night.

That leaves me wondering why in the world Lisa didn't go get her instead of having her struggle on and off a public bus, though.

"That's fine. It's fine." I respond. "It will probably be good for me to catch up with her." I'm already silently counting down the minutes until she leaves.

She puts her hand behind my head and pulls my face in to hers hard, giving me a quick and painful kiss.

"Thank you." Bending closer to me, she tells me softly, "This will all be over soon and we'll all be so happy forever."

She turns and walks back to the kitchen, leaving me with my mouth agape.

"Who's hungry?!" she yells.

"Me! Me! Me!" Tyler yells back.

I wait a moment before going back to the kitchen table. Her response was so strange. So happy forever? She sounds like she's in a trance, robotic almost. As I head back to the kitchen I wonder how I've been married to this woman and yet never told her about the relationship with my mother. Did she not notice that my mother and I don't speak? Was my mom even at the wedding? I can't remember it so I'm left to wonder. Whatever the reason I chose to keep this a secret from Lisa, it's very strange. A new mystery for me to figure out, as if I need another.

I expected there would be a lot of chatter at dinner, everyone catching up. Instead, it's relatively quiet, except for Tyler yammering on about this and that, and Lisa congratulating him on how well he is eating. The meal isn't that great, and I wonder if I'm just too distracted to enjoy it. My mom eats in silence, as if she's brooding over something. I feel the tension in the air and I'm not sure it if it's between my mom and Lisa, my mom and me, or possibly even Lisa and me.

"Anyone want some coffee?" Lisa asks, as we finish up.

"That would be great, thank you," I say. "Mom, coffee?"

My mother looks up and smiles as me. Lisa seems to take that as a yes, and starts a fresh pot. A few minutes later, she comes back to the table with a cup for each of us, along with cream and sugar.

"I can't recall how you like it." She looks to my mom. Collecting the plates from the table, she adds, "Why don't you guys go catch up a bit?"

"Sounds nice." I lie. "Thank you."

My mother stands up slowly, using the table for support. It makes me wonder why she isn't using her walker. I didn't even see that she brought one.

"I've only got one good hand here, but can I help you? " I ask her.

She brushes me off, a sense of tension already in the air

between us. She picks up her coffee, and starts walking across the dining room into the living room. I grab my cup and follow behind. As we make our way toward the couch, I ask how her trip was. She ignores me. I'm wondering if maybe she's hard of hearing and perhaps I've just forgotten that too.

Sitting on the couch, I notice that her hands are shaking. She puts her cup on the coffee table and motions for me to sit next to her. I do, and she puts her hand on my knee.

"Son, it's your mother," she says.

"I, umm... I remember who you are, Mom. My memory isn't totally gone. Just mostly gone," I say, trying to break the tension.

She looks at me, smiles a little, then looks away.

"I'm actually recovering well this time." I tell her, as if I still believe that. Looking closer at my mom, I'm wondering if she's actually doing okay. She seems out of it. Spaced out. Between her and Lisa's strange comments, and trance-like behaviors that seems to be contagious, I'm starting to wonder if something else is going on that I don't know about.

"I'm glad you're doing better," she replies. "I've been praying and praying. The good Lord listens, Stephen. I know you don't believe, but He does."

"Okay, Mom. Well, we can at least agree that I'm getting better, which is a good thing." I force myself to mentally step away from this part of the conversation with her because she believes what she believes, no matter how nonsensical it may be to me.

"We've all been staying strong for you. For each other," she says, and her voice drops down so softly that I can barely hear her. "You've got such a won...ser...."

Now I'm straining hard to hear her.

"What's that, Mom?" I ask.

"Can you hear me, Stephen?" She asks, speaking louder. She

is staring off into space, as if she sees something in the air. It's starting to scare me.

"I can hear you now, Mom. Are you okay?" I ask.

She turns and looks me straight in the face for a moment.

"You've got such a wonderful support system," she says, louder. Then her voice drops soft again and a thought suddenly occurs to me. Is she purposely saying some things softer so that Lisa can only hear part of the conversation?

"Yes, I do. I'm certainly thankful for that." I tell her, taking a sip of my coffee.

"We're not going to give up on you, Stephen. You'll make a full recovery, I know it." Her voice dropping a few decibels again, although still audible. "We are all praying. We need you, son. We all do, especially Haley," she whispers.

She said Haley.

Everything stops.

Haley's face pops up in my mind. This time, in great detail. Dark brown hair, almost black. Dark green eyes. A small scar on the edge of her bottom lip. She fell off a swing when she was four, and got a deep cut there.

Images start flashing through my mind:

Me and Haley in college, then at the park with the old chipped picnic table.

A picture of a hotel on the beach.

Us together in this house...in the bedroom.

Haley typing away at her desk, in Tyler's room.

Dozens of random images and thoughts of her start flipping through my mind, faster than I can catch them, like a movie on fast forward. She's caring, and sweet, and, compassionate. She loves peaches, and hates celery. She writes me little notes all the time and leaves them all over the house, even in my truck. She loves dogs, and she once surprised me by giving me one as a Christmans present. An image of Annie pops into my mind.

She's a marketing consultant and works tirelessly. She hates sleeping, and she reads at least one book a week. Her left pinky toe is crooked. She loves board games, but only the old ones that have been around for ages like Life and Monopoly. She can't stand "chick flicks" and prefers horror movies. She donates to charity every week, but prefers that no one know that. Her parents are still married. They live in San Jose, California. She maintains a great relationship with both of them. She loves dreamcatchers and has a tattoo of one down her left torso. She's allergic to bee stings. She is committed and faithful. She's tough as nails and rarely cries, but when she does, it's a big cry.

She...she's...beautiful, inside and out...and I love her. More than I've ever loved anyone or anything, I love her.

An image of Haley, standing beside me. We're outside of a church, in a courtyard. The church has a huge stained glass window of a sunrise. Haley is wearing a wedding dress...

I DROP my coffee flat on my lap, causing it to splash straight up my shirt, on my neck, and across the couch. Some of it gets on my mom, yet she doesn't even react.

"Owww!" I feel the coffee burning my skin.

Lisa comes running into the living room.

"Oh, shit!" She runs back out then returns with a small towel.

"Are you guys okay?" Grabbing my now-empty cup and sponging the coffee up off of my shirt and neck, she looks us both over. She pulls up my shirt. My skin is red, but not burned.

"Yikes, butterfingers," she says. "You guys really okay?"

"Yes. Sorry." I say, trying to hide the flood of memories that are coming back to me. My wife? Haley. I remember her. I remember my wedding. Suddenly, I feel a longing for her that is simply indescribable. I remember the science exhibit where she came to me. Where is she now?

Who is this woman, Lisa? Tyler? Why is everyone pretending that they are my family?

Lisa finishes wiping up the spilled coffee. My mom and I never move from our seats. My mom never even acknowledges that I spilled it or that Lisa is wiping it up off of her. It's as if her mind is somewhere else altogether. Lisa leaves again and comes back with a clean t-shirt. She helps me change shirts on the couch, then leaves me sitting here again with my mom.

"Mom?" I ask, purposely whispering now. "Who exactly is Haley? Where is she? What the hell is going on?"

She looks over at me. "I've got to get some rest, Stephen. Hang in there, son. I love you."

She struggles to get up.

"No..no...no!" I whisper and then as loudly as I can, "Who is she, Mom! Tell me that much now! I have to know!"

She finally stands all the way up, then waddles out to the kitchen again, completely ignoring my pleas for answers. A few moments later, Lisa comes in again, grabbing my mom's suitcase.

"I'll bring this to the spare room for her. You sure you're okay?" She asks, and I'm sure she notices the shock that must be written all over my face. I can't hide it.

"Yes. I'm just feeling really tired. I'm going to go lie down," I say, autonomously. I get up and head for the bedroom.

"I'll come check on you in a little while." She tells me, but I notice the suspicion on her face this time. It's very real and painfully obvious.

"You never did tell me what happened to the bottle caps and the painting," I remind her.

"Huh? What bottle caps and what painting?" She inquires, and I can't tell if she is serious or kidding. She pauses a moment, then turns and walks down the hall with the suitcase.

A million thoughts race through my head. Is Haley my ex-wife? Now my lover? Am I cheating on my wife with my ex-wife? Is Lisa really just pretending to be my wife? All of these questions are back, but this time I know they are real. She is real. None of this is in my head. I may be going crazy with the visions, but I know that Haley is real and so is—or was—my relationship with her. Lying back on the bed, I absolutely have to think of a way to find her again. To find out what's happened.

I get back out of the bed, and walk to the living room as quietly as I can. Tyler's bedroom door is shut, but I don't hear him in there. As I get to the living room, there's no sign of Lisa or my mom. Even Annie is absent. I walk over to the box of cards from the hospital again to chance peaking in it once more, but it's gone. Lisa either cleaned up to make things tidy before my mom got here, or she's hidden it from me. I'm suspecting the latter.

With no sign of anyone even in the house, I sit on the couch again. The coffee's been cleaned up, but the carpet in front of the couch is damp in a few spots. With all of these thoughts of Haley and Lisa in my head, I scan my mind, and the room, for any sign of what's going on. I need access to my memories, at all costs.

The coat closet.

The photo albums!

I get up as quickly as I can and rush over to the closet, expecting the albums to be gone as well. They aren't, and I grab them in my good arm and waddle back to the couch, trying not to drop them. I feel a perpetual need to rush, as Lisa could come walking in here at any moment. The first one I look through is the yellow one. The first picture, me and Annie in the pool. I study the picture as closely as I can. Nothing strange about it. Flipping through the pages one by one, I try to quickly study each picture. Me grilling burgers, my mom sitting by the pool, Annie rolling around in the grass. I notice that there aren't any pictures of Lisa or Tyler from this day. The next page is a picture of Tyler. He must have been about two in this picture. He's wearing overalls with no shirt on underneath, sitting up against a stuffed horse. This picture was done in a studio, with a professional photographer. I keep scanning the pictures. The next one looks newer, almost current. Tyler sitting in Lisa's lap in our living room, but this picture isn't quite right. The lighting is off. They're sitting in the light of the window, but the light on their faces is on the opposite side. It's as if they were superimposed into the picture.

I look up and listen closely. Still no sign of anyone. Where would they have gone at this time of night? My mom would not go for a walk with Annie and Lisa. She can barely walk without pain. A sense of concern is tugging at me, but I continue to study the pictures.

Looking back at the album, I turn the pages one by one. More pictures of Lisa and Tyler. Most of them in locations that are not familiar to me. A couple of images of them at local restaurants. I make it to the end of the album. No luck with any real clues.

Grabbing the red album, I scan the pictures of me as a child. Still no luck and no memories from it. I don't see anything strange either, unless I count my dad in the background looking so concerned, but...Wait.

He looks...different.

He's smiling right at the camera. I go back to the beginning of the album, thinking I've somehow missed the pictures of him with that strained look on his face. One by one, I go through the pictures again, taking my time. The pictures I recall with my dad looking off into the distance, grief stricken, are instead pictures of him looking right at the camera with a big smile on his face. Am I remembering this incorrectly? Have some pictures been replaced. Am I really slipping and losing my mind?

The last album, the white one, only confirms that I must indeed be going insane. 'We Don't Remember The Days, We Remember The Moments' printed on the front, as if to mock me. From the first page on, the random pictures of places with no people are still there, just as before. But now, Haley is in almost all of them. The beach picture has her standing forefront, in the sand. The picture of the old grey picnic table, it's the one from my dream. Haley up close, smiling at the camera. Smiling at me. The picture of the windmill has Haley in it, sitting off to the side. I flip a few pages further this time to find a picture of Haley and me together. The first one is us in a fake jail cell. The kind at all the tourist traps. We're both smiling...no, laughing. The camera is off a bit and you can see over the jail door, a line of shops aligning a street. A pier in the far background. It looks like a boardwalk. The next few pictures appear to be from that same boardwalk. Haley trying on a ridiculously large hat. Me standing behind a wooden cutout of a headless, overly muscular body. My head the only thing showing, as if to give the illusion that I'm the muscle man. The next page hits me the hardest. Haley, standing out on the pier. She has a huge smile on her face and her cheeks are wet, as if she's been crying. I remember this! She was so happy. I was so nervous that day. She's holding her left hand up for the camera to show off an engagement ring.

Sitting here now, I hear Lisa. She's yelling something to the neighbors about the weather being so nice. She's in the front yard. I shut the album and rush to stack them so I can carry them to the closet. I'll never make it there and back to the bed before she comes in. As quickly as I can, I carry the stack of albums in my good arm. Just as I'm at the closet door, I hear the front door opening. Putting the albums back, the white one falls from my arm and lands open on a page of Haley in a store. She's wearing a wedding dress. I lean down and grab the album, shutting it and putting in on the top of the stack as fast as I can. Lisa is in the house now. I hear her fiddling with Annie's leash. Closing the closet door as gently and quietly as I can, I move into the kitchen and grab a coffee cup from the hook on the wall.

"Steve, is that you?" Lisa calls out.

"Yeah. It's me. What's up?" I say, trying my hardest to sound casual as I fill the cup with water from the sink. I feel a bead of sweat traveling down the middle of my back.

"I thought you went to bed. Is something wrong?" she asks, and her acting is worse than mine. She is absolutely aware that something else is going on.

"No, I'm fine. Just getting some water, that's all."

The photo album pictures are on a rolling loop in my head. Maybe my brain was damaged before the surgery and I wasn't seeing the pictures as they really are. That's the only explanation that makes any sense to me, although I'm not sure it really makes sense at all. But now I remember that one day, proposing to Haley. I could happily drown in the memories of that day as they come to me, but not right now. Now it's time to see how much of a game is being played here, to see what information I can get from Lisa.

"My mind is playing tricks on me, I think. Can I ask you something?" I ask, walking out of the kitchen.

Lisa has the leash off of Annie, and she's taking off her sneakers by the door.

"Of course." I can tell she's worried, but not about me. She's worried that she is going to be exposed for whatever she is doing here.

I clear my throat a couple of times, yet it's still dry and my voice comes out scratchy. "Was I married before?"

The look of shock on her face gives her away before she can say a word.

"Before what?" She tries to sound ambiguous, unsuccessfully.

"Was I married to someone else before you and I got married? Do I have an ex-wife?" The pointedness of my question giving away my aggravation.

"Not that you ever made me aware of, no." She interjects. "You sound hoarse. Are you sure you're not coming down with something?" She asks, clearly trying to change the subject.

A sudden urge to show Lisa the photo album comes to me, but I refrain. The pictures don't technically show that I was married, and even if they did, a little part of me is afraid that the moment I go to show Lisa, they'll change back into pictures without anyone in them. I decide to take a different approach.

"I am fine. I guess it just seems odd to me that my own mom, who I never see, tells me that... " I start to say, but my voice cracks again. I really do need some more water. Lisa walks right past me and into the kitchen while I'm in mid-sentence.

"Hang on." She calls from the kitchen. "I'm going to get you some hot tea. You sound horrible, like you have a cold or something."

She's right. My throat is dry, but I know she is stalling. Trying to change the subject. If Haley is my ex-wife, or my ex-lover, or girlfriend, or whatever...Lisa is trying to prevent me from remembering. I walk over and sit down on the couch. I'm sitting there in the silence of my thoughts for what seems like forever, when Lisa finally comes back in. She's carrying a fancy little white and gold teacup with a teabag in it. Looking at her, I can't take the deception any more.

"Let's be clear here." I call her out. "You are hiding something from me. Maybe a lot of things. I know it and so do you."

"Steve. Listen to me." She finally admits, "You are right. I've not been one hundred percent honest, and for that, I am truly sorry. I'm just...scared." She sets the tea down on the side table.

"I put honey in this. It'll help your throat. I'm having trouble listening to your voice like that. It sounds painful and scratchy."

I sit up, taking the teacup from her and have a few sips. It's warm and sweet, and it does make my throat feel better.

"Sit down." I don't ask. "I need to know exactly what it is you've been keeping from me." My voice returning to normal, the scratchiness now gone.

"Well..." She sits down next to me and starts wringing her hands. "Our past relationship was not without its problems. We were happy. We were in love. You loved me so much. You did." She says. "So much..." She sits still, not saying anything more.

I take a few more sips of the tea to coat my throat. This simple act seems to diminish some of the hostility of the conversation. "And?" I ask, a little more calmly.

"And...nothing. We were happy. In love." She repeats.

"So what is it that you're keeping from me? " I ask. "Are you really going to make me pull it from you one bit at a time?"

"No...no. You're right." She replies. "See, even though we were happy, and you loved me... There is always someone on the outside who is jealous of that, and tries to mess it up."

I take another sip of tea, then set the cup back down. "So, someone interfered with our marriage?" I ask.

"No, someone *tried* to interfere. Someone is still trying to." She explains.

Suddenly, I feel a wave of exhaustion come over me. I lie back on the couch.

"Who? Tell me who? Who is this person?" I demand.

"What does it matter?!" She's getting upset. Her voice is getting louder, yet it seems further away. Like I'm falling down a hole. I strain to hear her.

"You look exhausted. Let's get you to bed." She tells me, and she's right. I am. I sit and go to stand, feeling a wave of dizziness come over me. I almost fall down. Lisa takes my arm and gently pulls me up and walks with me down the hall, to the bedroom.

"It does matter. It matters because I want the truth." I expect the truth from my own *wife*. You think we can just reset our relationship because I can't remember? We will never have a real relationship until we start from the beginning. From the truth. No secrets. No games. No more lies." I'm trying to shout, but I can hardly hear my own voice. All of my energy is escaping with each word. Lisa guides me into the bedroom and helps me into the bed.

"It's time for the truth, Lisa. The real truth!" My shouts are whispers.

I feel myself falling asleep when I realize...I've been drugged. The tea.

"The truth?" She says, and now she's angry, yet she's getting eerily calm. She stands up, towering over me. I try to move but I can't.

She smiles. "You don't want the truth. No, not that." Now fully enraged, she starts yelling, and as I slip closer to sleep, she somehow continues to get louder.

"You're not after the truth! You just want your precious Haley back. You just want to leave me all alone again." Well, newsflash, Mr. Lewis, Mr. High and Mighty, Mr. Brainiac Big Shot Engineer, that's not happening again. Not now. Not ever. You are mine now. You said you love me. You said it and so it's true. You can't take that back!"

She knows about Haley. I knew it.

I can't fight the sleep any longer. She keeps talking but now I can't hear it. Just as sleep takes me, I realize something else.

She called me an engineer.

24

Then nothing. Black. Silent.

MY BODY FEELS heavy and weighed down. I try to raise my arms but, no matter how hard I try, they simply won't move. I try to speak but nothing comes out and I realize that my voice is completely gone. Little patterns of light dance across my closed eyelids, but they won't open. From far away, I can hear distant voices chattering but I can't tell what they are saying. Someone is holding my hand. Their skin is smooth and feminine. It's a woman. I smell her perfume. It has a hint of jasmine and this reminds me of her. I miss her. She's whispering now, close. I can almost feel her lips on my ear, her breath soft and warm. "I love you."

But the voice.

It's different this time.

It's not her.

It's Lisa.

I open my eyes to her face, hovering right over mine.

"I love you, Steve. I love you. I love you. I love you." She repeats, and her breath stinks. "...and you love me too. You told me so. I knew it. I could tell."

I try to raise my arms again but they won't move. Even my good hand. Nothing. I look down and see why. My legs and right hand are handcuffed to thick black cables attached to the bed. My right arm still in the sling.

"What?...What are you doing?!" I scream. "Help! Somebody help me! Somebody help me!" Over and over again I yell it, as loud as I can. I scream it again and again.

She reaches in her back pocket and pulls out a Bowie knife. It's leathery brown handle looks old and used. The knife is huge. I try with all of my strength to move. To break free, but it's useless. I can't move an inch. I'm fastened to the bed tightly. She reaches down and presses the tip of the knife against my crotch. I feel the little pin prick of it against me.

"Are you sure you want to yell like that?" She asks, calmly.

I stop yelling, still looking down. A small dot of blood spreads across the crotch of my pants.

"No. No. I...I'm sorry." I stopped yelling. "Lisa. You...you just scared me. Why...why am I tied up?" I whisper, trying not to all out panic.

She puts the knife on the side table.

"You just had to keep pushing, didn't you? You couldn't just be happy with me. With Tyler." She paces back and forth around the bed.

"We can't be a family without you, Steve. Not anymore. Not after what you did to us. If you won't stay, then I'll make sure you have no choice. You can stay here and sleep with me forever." Her voice sounding guttural, almost like a growl.

"You put me in the position, Steve, because without you, I am truly alone. I won't be alone again, not after what you said.

You said you loved me. You said that. Why would you say that?" she asks.

"I do love you." I lie. "I...I just wanted to know why I keep getting these strange memories. Memories that made no sense. If...If you would have just told me about all of that other stuff, I could stop wondering and live my life with you. You and Tyler. Happy."

I'm desperate and I'll say anything to survive this. To get back to Haley.

"You...you do?" She asks, and for a moment she looks sad. Her lip starts to quiver.

"Yes. Of course I do."

"Do you remember us?" She asks. "Do you remember me? Our son?"

"I remember parts of you and Tyler. I just need a little more time. But I do. I remember you and how much you love me and how much I love you. I want so bad to remember everything about us. I'm trying." I'm yammering on with my lies. She must be able to tell.

"Why do you need to remember anything else about us? As long as you remember how much you love us. Why does anything else matter?" She stops, looking down at me, almost accusing me of wanting to dig up something bad about her or Tyler.

"It...I suppose it doesn't. I just wanted to recall things we've done. Our wedding. So we can reminisce some times. You know?" I ask. I'm starting to panic after all. I can feel the sweat beads on my forehead.

"We don't need to think about the past, Steve. We need to focus on now and our future. You need to let the past go. It's stopping you from enjoying your family. Your family needs you, Steve. I need you." She seems to go soft for a moment, the anger in her eyes fading.

"I know. I'm sorry. I was being selfish. I will let it go. I want to focus on us. Now. Right now. Our life together. Our...our future."

"Good. I agree. Let's get your mind clear of anything else." She stands up and relaxes her grip on the knife.

"Do you want some breakfast?" she asks, and I know that I need to answer affirmative to keep her pacified for now. To prevent her from getting angrier.

"Sure. That sounds nice." I tell her, my mind already scanning for how I can get her to release me.

"Eggs and bacon?" she asks.

"Just what I was thinking," I reply.

"Okay. I'll be just a few minutes." She walks toward the door.

"Lisa, are you going to untie me?" I ask, not knowing how she'll react to this question.

"Oh, honey, I'll untie you soon. Once we've made sure you're all better. Once I know that you're able to focus on your family. Soon." She leans over and kisses me on the lips, jamming her stinking tongue in my mouth for a moment. Then, she turns and walks out of the room.

ALONE IN THE ROOM, I wait. I assess that Lisa has had time to get to the kitchen when I risk raising my left arm as high as I can. The pain is unbearable and I immediately lower my arm back down. I'm trapped, yet the cold dark fear that fills my mind is not for me. My mother. Where is she? What has Lisa done to her? I try to pull my right arm free of the handcuff but it won't budge. The cuffs are tight and the black cables look impossible to break. The complexity of the manner in which she's tied me up tells me that she's had this ready as a backup plan, should I discover that she's a fraud. The cables are all precut and pre-connected to the handcuffs. I'm stuck here with no way out.

Thoughts of Haley fill my mind again. Is she my wife? Who

is Lisa? How do I remember being here in this house before the accident? Why is my mom here? Has Lisa somehow tricked her too? Why did she call me an engineer? None of this makes any sense. I have a million loop holes in anything that I come up with. I'm lost and without any direction or notion of what my life really was before the accident, I openly weep.

I hear footsteps coming down the hall. I'm almost wishing it were some sort of ghost or invisible force, like before. But I know it's Lisa, I can hear her humming, as if it's just another day at home. She pushes the door open with her foot, and carries in a tray. She's made a nicely placed breakfast of eggs and bacon for me. It's all displayed on the fine china, with a perfectly folded napkin, fork, and a tall glass of orange juice. I wonder if she's drugged the food or the juice, but I have no choice but to eat it now anyway.

She sits down on the bed next to me.

"What's wrong, babe? You've been crying." She looks me over, as if this is all perfectly normal and I have no reason to be anything but happy to be here.

"I just...I don't know how we got here. I want us to be back to normal. I don't want to be tied here like this. My arm hurts in this position. I...I just want things back like they were, like we were. I just want you back." My lies are so thick in my mouth, I can almost taste them.

"I'm so sorry, babe. I really am. I'll get you some pain pills, but I can't let you up yet. I have to be sure. I can't risk losing you after all we've been through together. It can't all be for nothing." She says, cutting up eggs with the side of the fork.

"Can you eat, or do I need to get you some pills first?" she asks.

I don't want any more drugs right now. I need to think clearly. I respond.

"I can eat. The pills make me nauseous on an empty stomach

anyway. But, I'm not sure how I'll eat lying down." I ask her, hoping she'll see the dilemma for what it is.

She places the tray on the floor and grabs the extra pillows laying around. Gently, she pushes two small pillows under my head and upper back, tilting me upward, but not quite sitting me upright.

"There, that should help," she says, and sits back down with the tray.

"Open up." She brings the egg-filled fork to my lips.

I open my mouth and let her feed me, one bite after the other, until I've eaten everything.

"Drink some water, babe. You've got to be thirsty." She brings the glass to my mouth.

I reach out with my lips for the glass, taking a couple of gulps. This is how I suspect she'll drug me with the sleeping pills again, if she wants me to stay put. She pulls the glass away.

"More?"

I shake my head no.

"How long before you think you can trust me?" I ask.

"Oh, it's not that I can't trust you, Steve. I just need to make sure you're no longer confused. That's all. I know your heart is in the right place. I know that. You told me and I could feel it. But confusing thoughts and memories can mess things up for us. For you." She looks back down to my crotch where the little prickle of dried blood remains, a not-so-gentle reminder of the power she has over me.

"When I'm sure you're all better, I'll let you go." She leans in to kiss me on the lips again, and I'm disgusted by it. Disgusted by her lies and the measures she's taken to keep me. I'm starting to realize that I am not the crazy one after all. I hold my breath and kiss her back.

She stands up with the tray and puts it on the dresser.

"Where's my mom, Lisa?" I ask, point blank.

"She left first thing this morning, babe." Lisa smiles, and although a smiles plays on the edges of her lips it's menacing all the same. "She wanted to say goodbye but I told her you had a nasty hangover from a little too much wine last night. I don't think she approved. She seemed a little angry when she left."

"Wow, that seems a little mean," I say, trying to sound wounded but really happy my mom is gone from this house and away from this crazy woman.

"Here," she says, grabbing the TV remote. "Why don't you watch something. Maybe it'll help you pass the time for a while." She turns on the TV, then grabs the tray again and heads for the door.

"Wait." I say, "What about Tyler? Won't he think this is kind of strange? Dad tied to the bed? What if he tells someone? Or are you going to keep him from me for a while? I don't want that," I say, hoping to play on her desire for me to want to see Tyler.

"You're silly, Steve. Tyler is smart. He understands what's going on. He won't risk anything that might jeopardize his family. He's lost so much already in his short little life. He knows what real loss is, Steve. He wants you to stay at all costs. He's growing to like you." She smiles and walks out with the tray.

She left the TV blaring, as if she's trying to cover up the noise of something else in the house. Again, I worry about my mom. Did she really leave? Lisa is back almost immediately, this time with a bottle of water and a couple of pain pills in her hand.

"Let's get you more comfortable," she says. "Open up."

I do, and she drops the pills on my tongue. She pushes the water bottle up to my mouth and makes me take a couple of drinks. I try to catch the pills with my tongue to cheek them but it's no use and I swallow them down.

"There." Smiling, she pulls the bottle away. She stands up

and gently removes the extra pillows from behind my head and back, leaving me lying flat again.

"You should feel much better soon. I'll come check on you a little later. I've got to run a few errands. I'm taking Tyler and Annie so you can get some rest," she adds.

Before I can think of a reply, she walks out and closes the door, still leaving the TV turned up too loud.

Sitting here now, I have nothing to do but think. The volume on the television interrupts my thoughts and just as I'm getting used to it, the pain pills kick in, making me feel sleepy again. I try to fight it, forcing my eyes open. Looking at the TV, I see it's a talk show. The host is sitting behind a desk with two guests sitting alongside it on a couch. My eyes are going blurry and I'm straining to focus when the channels change. Then changes again, and again. I strain my eyes to see the remote sitting on the dresser in front of the bed, yet the channels keep changing. My first thought is that the TV is faulty, but in light of everything I've experienced lately, I know that there is nothing wrong with the TV. Straining as hard as I can to stay awake, the channels stop flipping on a show about animals. A lion is chasing a zebra across a field of high grass. It's all in slow motion, and underneath the narrator's voice, I hear someone else's voice.

"You into nature shows?" An older woman's voice.

"Nah...not really. There's just nothing on." Another woman's voice. It's fading as I'm falling asleep again. "I'm not really watching anyway."

I recognize this woman's voice.

It's Haley.

I wake to Lisa walking back into the bedroom. Looking down, I'm still tied securely to the bed. As I'm shaking off the dream of the television and of Haley, my mind quickly switches to any way I might get Lisa to let me go. Nothing I think of seems feasible.

"Good morning, sleepy head. You've slept the whole morning away." She says, with a big, cheerful grin on her face, as if I could have been doing anything else after being tied up and drugged.

"Yeah, those painkillers put me to sleep," I say.

"I know, that's what I put in your tea yesterday, just double the normal dose." Proudly, still smiling, as if she thinks this is a fun game for us to play together.

"You hungry again? I made homemade chicken soup," she adds.

"Well, kind of. My body feels so stiff like this," I say, but she doesn't acknowledge my physical discomfort.

"Soup or no?" she asks.

"Sure...yeah. I guess you'll need to feed it to me again. Hold the drugs, unless they're cooked right in," I say and I'm starting to feel angry.

"Soup, it is, and I didn't put drugs in it. Your sarcasm isn't going to get you unchained any sooner," she scoffs, walking out.

I wiggle back and forth, checking my restraints. Everything is still tight. There's got to be a way to get free. If I have to lie here in this prison for too long, I feel like I'll go crazy, if I'm not already. I blink away the sleepy feeling still lingering, and take inventory of my situation. Now that I've had the surgery, I'm still seeing visions and things that aren't there, or...at the very least...things that are impossible. Changing photos, footsteps and voices, and let's not forget the invisible hand that grabbed my wrist. None of it makes any sense. Writhing back and forth on the bed again, I attempt to loosen any of the restraints or even parts of the bed, but nothing works. I'm stuck. Being nice does not seem like it's going to help me to get out of this, and I don't think I can keep the charade going for days on end, hoping she comes around. I'd rather have her just kill me and get it over with. The thought of what she's done to me...what seemingly impossible steps she must have done to execute this, it stirs up more anger in me.

"Okay, babe, soup's up!" Lisa bellows out, walking in, stopping me in mid-thought.

"You know, I've been lying here thinking of what kind of person would tie someone up to prevent them from leaving," I say, my words building on my own anger.

"Oh, really." Setting the tray down on the night stand, the anger in her eyes building. "What kind of person did you conclude that is, Steve?" she asks. "Do tell."

"Oh, that's an easy answer." Looking over at the tray, I notice a bowl of soup, a glass of water, a napkin, a spoon, and a half full package of saltine crackers twisted shut with a twist tie. Suddenly, I know I need to back off.

"A person who would tie someone up to keep them from leaving obviously wants to keep their family together. That's the kind of person who would do anything for their family and the people they love," I say, backpedaling as fast as I can. "That's the kind of person I want to be with." I say. "...and I owe you an apology for starting to get upset. I'm just...I'm tired of being tied up, but I understand why you feel you need to keep me like this for a while. It's okay," I say, hoping she takes my charade as sincerity.

She says nothing for a few minutes and I'm sure I oversold it. I'm half expecting her to bring out her giant knife again when she says:

"Thank you, Steve, and you're right. That is the kind of person I am. I so want to let you go, to feel you up against me. This is torture for me too. But it will be worth it, for both of us. Trust me, it will. Let's just focus on getting you better." She reminds me, yet again.

"Let's do that," I say. "The soup smells delicious. Can I eat now?" I ask.

"Of course." She says, walking over to get the extra pillows and put them behind my head again. She sits down on the bed and begins feeding me soup. After a few spoonfuls, I ask for crackers. She opens the package, untwisting the tie and feeds me crackers. One at a time.

"That's so good. Thank you. A drink? Those crackers are salty. Good, but salty." I add, so as not to offend her.

She puts the glass to my lips and I drink, as fast as I can. Gulping down the water. She pulls the glass away, assuming I'm done.

"Sorry, a little more water? I think those pills give me cotton mouth too or something." I say.

"Of course. Yeah, maybe so," she replies, and tilts the glass to my lips again. I gulp down the water until it's gone.

She puts the glass down and starts feeding me soup again. I feel like my stomach is filled to the top with water, and I don't want any more soup, but I keep eating it anyway. A few more bites in and I interrupt again for a bite of cracker. She complies with a smile, then goes for the soup again.

"You're going to think I'm a giant pain, babe." I say. "But can I get a little more water? The crackers are killing me."

"Haha. You are a giant pain, but I love you all the same." She smiles and leans is to kiss my lips. "Sure, I'll be right back."

She grabs the glass and stands up. Heading for the bathroom, my hope fades. Then she turns and heads for the bedroom door instead.

"I'll be back in a sec," she calls.

As soon as she's a few steps down the hall, I move fast. Taking a few deep breaths, then one giant one and holding it in, I reach up with my broken arm. The pain is like hot lava in my arm and I suddenly feel like I need to pee. I can't take it any more and I lower my arm back down. She'll be back any second. This is my only chance. I take another breath and hold it in. All at once, I pull my arm out of the sling and reach over to the food tray. The pain is unbearable. My ears are ringing and I feel warm urine on the crotch of my pants. It slightly distracts me from the pain for a second. With my broken hand, I grab the twist tie that's still lying there by the food bowl then bring my arm back down into the sling in one fell swoop.

A tear runs down my cheek and I try to blow it away with my mouth. I hear her walking back down the hall towards me. She's seconds away.

"Sorry about that. The filtered water thing takes forever," she explains. "Oh my goodness! Are you alright?"

"Yeah. Yeah. I'm good," I say, my voice cracking.

"What the hell happened?" she asks.

"I...I was choking. You didn't hear me calling for you?" I ask.

"Oh, Steve. I'm so sorry. No, I didn't hear you. Here, take a drink." She tilts the water into my mouth and I take two gulps for good measure.

"Ahh. Thank you. I was dying here." I say, and it felt like it. Most of the sharp pain in my arm has subsided. Now it's a dull throb.

"You have a little accident there on your pants," she points out.

"Huh?" I look down, faking surprise. "Oh, jeez. That's embarrassing." I notice it's only a small spot. "I didn't want to complicate things here, but I really have to pee. How are we going to work that?" I ask.

"I have a handheld urinal, silly." She sets the water down and goes into the closet.

She has a handheld urinal? Of course she does. She did plan this out, after all. Coming back out, she's holding a clear plastic handheld urinal by its handle.

"I'm going to have to hold it for you. It won't be the first time," she says, and winks at me.

"What if I have to...umm...really go. Like more than just pee?" I ask.

"Then I'll scoot the bedpan under you and leave you for a few minutes for privacy." She has this all figured out, apparently.

The bedpan? It makes me wonder what other contraptions she has handy in case she needs to keep someone prisoner in the house.

"Well, I just need to pee," I say, trying to fake a little smile.

She unzips my pants and pulls them down a little, then grabs me and tucks me into the opening on the plastic urinal. For a moment I'm afraid I don't really need to pee, or can't now, and she'll know I was lying. But then everything starts flowing and I've filled the thing half way up by the time I stop.

"There you go. All done." She tells me, and heads to the bathroom to dump the urinal out.

I squeeze the twist tie in my hand, making sure I still have it. It's there, and with it, my only chance of getting out of here.

25

I 've been lying here for what seems like hours. Lisa comes and goes to check on me. She turned the television on and left it for me to watch. I notice that it's on a nature show about animals. Did she change it to this channel, or was it on this channel when she powered it on? I think of my latest dream again for a moment. Assuming each show is thirty minutes to any hour, I'm never left alone for more than about twenty minutes at a time. Although my acting seemed to pacify her at the time, she doesn't trust me. She's been in here to give me water, adjust the pillows, turn up the television, and even urinal duty a couple of times. But her visits are really to make sure I'm still tied up and still behaving. Of this, I have no doubt.

"How you doing?" she asks, walking back in, as if she hasn't seen me a dozen time already today.

"I'm hanging in there," I reply.

"Well, I hate to leave you, but my car is finally fixed. My mom is dropping by to give me a ride to go get it. I won't be gone long." Her explanation of where she is going makes me wonder if this is a test.

Why would she give me specifics like that? So I'd think she'll be gone for a while? So she can see if I try anything? I'm still tightly gripping onto this twist tie. It feels like some sort of life raft now, yet I don't know how I'm actually going to use it to escape. My broken arm is sore, but the throbbing has stopped. I've not mentioned being uncomfortable or in pain because I don't want any more pain pills. I need to be sharp when the opportunity presents itself, and it will come. Maybe today. This thought is keeping me going.

"Okay, babe, I'll miss you," I add, again hoping I'm not laying it on too thick.

"Aww. I'll miss you too, but I'll be back in a jiffy," she replies, walking over to give me another quick kiss, then turning and walking out.

I lie here, listening for any signs of her leaving, but hear none. The television volume makes it hard to hear much beyond this room. As I've been watching the shows, if only to measure time, I've been half expecting the television to start changing channels again. Apparently, it is no longer haunted, or at least not for now. The station hasn't changed and I don't hear any voices except those of the narrators on the various shows. It makes me wonder if I was having some kind of reaction to the drugs or whatever else Lisa may have given me. Then, it occurs to me that this could explain all of the visions I've seen. If Lisa's been drugging me this whole time. The idea comes and goes just as quickly because it has too many holes for me to be able to validate it in any way. Am I becoming the crazed madman who is constantly thinking some bizarre conspiracy and then acting on it? Next, I'll be wanting to wear a foil helmet to prevent the aliens from reading my thoughts. A joke, but one that reminds me to stay in check of my own thoughts. I take a deep breath. Everything is going to be fine and I'm going to get out of this, I tell myself.

Afternoon turns to evening and I notice it getting darker

outside the window. Lisa hasn't been back in here in over two hours this time, and a new fear creeps into my head for a moment. What if something happened to her? What if she fell, or got into a car accident, or even offed herself? I'd be left here to starve to death. A slow and painful death, I'm sure. I look at the television, trying to remember when this show started. This one is about sea life. A transparent, squid-like creature swims past a group of divers. Should I attempt to escape now? Am I risking her coming back in here? Of course I am. Is this a trick? If I blow this, she'll be more careful in preventing me from getting another opportunity. Knowing this, I also know that means I'm only going to get one shot at escape. My intention has been to wait for her to run an errand, but I'm afraid she'll drug me if she has to leave me for too long. So far, I haven't had a chance to try anything. I close my eyes for a moment and decide to take action now.

FOLDING the twisty tie twice with my broken hand proves to be more painful than I had expected. Once I have it folded, I discover that twisting the folded tie with one hand, even if it weren't a broken hand, is very difficult. It takes longer than I expected, and I'm immediately regretting that I did not do this part hours ago. Once I get the tie folded and twisted, it's more sturdy and does not bend as easily. Taking another deep breath, I prepare for the immense pain that's coming. Again, in one big movement, I take my hand out of the sling and raise my arm upwards, the pain comes back worse than I remembered from before. Tears build in my eyes already. Crossing my broken arm across my face shifts the pain a little for a moment, then it comes on even stronger. I'm just bearing the pain when I realize the inevitable. I cannot reach my right wrist with my broken left arm. It simply will not raise up that far without causing me to pass out from the exertion. My pain threshold is only so high.

I lower my arm back down to my waist and take a breath. The pain in my arm is still screaming, but I feel it slowly starting to fade a little. One more try, that's all I've got in me. Holding my breath once more, I raise my broken arm up to my right wrist. An explosion of pain in my left shoulder but this time, I reach the handcuff on my right hand.

Sticking the twist tie into the key hole of the handcuff isn't as tricky as I had thought it would be, but the pain is growing by the second. It's making me sweat and my hands are getting slippery. I attempt a quick turn of the twist tie in the lock hole. No luck. I've only got a few seconds left before I have to let go. The pain is too much. I try once more and the twist tie slips out of my hand and falls out of the handcuff. It skips off the headboard, then falls down the crack at the top of the mattress. I hear it hit the hardwood floor under the bed. I lower my arm and realize that was it. My only chance. I'm now stuck here until she lets me up, if that ever happens.

I spend the next thirty minutes or so lying there, staring at the ceiling and waiting for the pain to go away. It never does, although it does lessen enough to allow me to breathe normally. Taking a few deep breaths in through my mouth and out through my nose. I'm in a tolerable amount of pain now but physically, I'll make it. Mentally, I'm not quite so sure. I would rather die than lie here for another night. Waiting and wondering and scared. I close my eyes and hope against hope that another idea or any opportunity presents itself.

The timing in between shows is perfect as the silent gap on the television allows me to hear a car door closing in the driveway. A few minutes later, Lisa walks in. She's carrying a brown paper bag and a paper cup with a straw in it.

"Hey, sleepy head. How about a cheeseburger and a choco-late shake?" she asks, as if it's the greatest thing ever.

"That sounds amazing!" I say, with an accidental overly excited sounding burst, brought on by the new pain I get when speaking. The spike of pain travels down my broken arm and fades the moment I stop talking.

"Whoa there, sir. It's good, but it's not THAT good." She smiles like she's very satisfied with her level of wit.

She opens the bag and pulls a wax paper wrapping out. Opening the burger half way, she holds it down to my mouth.

"Wait, let's get you set up." Grabbing the pillows and prop-ping my head up again, she grabs the TV remote and clicks it off. "There. All set."

Taking a few napkins from the bag and laying them under my neck, she holds the burger down to my mouth. I take a big bite and chew. It might be amazing but I can't really taste it over the pain in my arm and the dawning shock of my situation.

"How was your day?" I ask, in between bites, as if this is a normal environment for casual conversation, the pain shooting up again with my question,

"It was really good. How about you? Learn anything cool on these shows?" She inquires, and sounds like a parent asking a kid about school.

"A few things. This is an interesting channel." I tell her, lacking any real response since I've not paid attention to the TV, and enduring the pain of each sentence with a happy face is all that I can manage.

"Can I have a drink of the shake?" I ask, trying not to wince.

"Of course. It's amazing." She quirks, using my own word back at me, as she tilts the cup down to my mouth. The lid pops off and freezing cold chocolate ice cream pours on my face, drip-ping down my neck. It distracts me from the pain in my arm for a second, but it also reminds me of how pathetic I am tied to the bed like this.

"If you'd just untie me from this bed, I could eat like a man and not like some fucking toddler you have to spoon feed!" I shout, before I even realize what I've said, the pain joining in to raise my voice even more.

She puts the shake down and walks into the bathroom. Coming back out, she wipes up my face and neck with a towel.

"You're right, Steve. You're absolutely right." Calmly, she sits down on the bed beside me. Looking directly at me for a moment, she says, "You were good today. Trustworthy. Maybe in a week or so we can try untying you. But if you keep getting angry with me, we're going to have problems, Steve. We don't want to have problems." She smiles at me, a menacing smile that tells me something that should have been obvious to me by now.

She is more than just a little disturbed. This woman is off-the-deep-end crazy, and if my situation does not change soon, it's quite likely that I will die here, in this bed.

"I understand and you are actually right. I'm sorry. I'm just so tired of being like this. I just want to go back to normal," I practically beg, the pain in my arm not letting up.

"So do I, Steve, and we will in good time."

"Where's Tyler?" I ask, feigning interest.

"He's out with my mom. He'll be home soon, but...I'd rather him not see you like this unless he has to. I'd rather you get better first." As if to remind me that my freedom and any chance at escaping is completely at her mercy.

"So, you're not going to let me see him for another week?" I ask.

"We all have to make sacrifices for the betterment of our family," she replies, as she gathers up the remnants of my meal.

"I understand." I say, not sure of what to add. This woman is obviously disturbed beyond any rational conversation.

I know it's getting late, but I have to run one more quick errand and then I'll be back. You gonna be fine for now? Do you need to go to the bathroom?" she asks, arching her brow my way reminding me that it's not only my freedom that's at her mercy, but my dignity, as well.

"You're going to let me go to the bathroom?" I ask.

"No, I meant...you know what I meant. Do you need to relieve yourself?" she asks.

"No. I'm good. Thanks," I reply.

"Okay, I'll be back before Tyler gets here. Get some more rest." She kisses me on the cheek.

As she's walking out the door, I wonder what errand she'd have to run this late. She shuts the bedroom door behind her and I'm left with the silence of this room and the throbbing pain in my arm. I can faintly here her in the kitchen, then silence. I few moments later, I hear the garage door open. We don't park in the garage, so I'm curious. Maybe she got her car back and parks it in there? Something tells me that there's a more sinister reason, and suddenly, my concern for my mom spikes into a cold fear, drenching me in its grip as I lie helpless in this bed. I listen intently and hear only silence. What seems like a long time later, I hear a car door (trunk?) slam, then another. The noise of a car starting, and then driving away. Lying here, listening as hard as I can, I hear all the little noises of the house. The occasional creaking of the house settling, the ice maker in the refrigerator as it breaks ice into the bin. The gut-wrenching fear for my mom expands to include Haley. Where is she? Did Lisa find her and...hurt her? I push back the thoughts of my mom or Haley being hurt, or worse. I need to figure out how I'm going to get out of here. There has to be a way. I'm going to have to try and use my arm again. I start to take slow, deep breaths, preparing myself for the pain. I briefly wonder if I'm doing permanent damage to something deep in my arm and rationalize that my freedom is worth the possibility. It sure feels like I've done more damage to it though. One more deep breath and I hold it in. Here goes nothing. I start to pull my arm out of the sling when the phone rings, scaring me so badly that I lurch, pulling the handcuff and the connected black cable taught against the bed frame. It doesn't budge. Waiting for the phone to stop ringing, I hear an answering message come on in the kitchen.

You have reached the Lewis family, and the Living Color home office. If you've reached this message, no one is available to take your call. Please leave a message including your name and phone number, and we'll be sure to call you back as soon as possible. Thank you.

The message ends and after a few clicks, I hear my mom's voice on the speaker.

"Steve, it's your mother. I just want you to know that I'm here for you, and that I'm praying for you, son. I...I guess I...(mumbling)...I just want you to know that I love you and... "

She's silent for so long, the answering machine times out and cuts her off.

Knowing that my mom is back home almost makes me feel foolish for thinking that Lisa had hurt her, until I look back down at my legs, handcuffed to the bed. I breathe a tremendous sigh of relief for my mom's safety, before I prepare to move my arm again. I have no idea of what I'm going to do. I have no plan, but I have to try. Preparing to move my arm is interrupted again when I hear the front doorknob jiggle and then open and shut. I hear footsteps in the foyer and I can tell by the speed of them that it's Tyler. Listening closely, his are the only footsteps I hear. He is coming down the hall. Then, I hear a door open in the hall. He's going to his room. I have to act fast before he shuts himself in there. I yell before I even think of what to say.

"Tyler! Tyler! It's Daddy! Can you come in my room for a minute?!" I yell as loud as I can, sending a shrieking pain through my arm and back. I pray that Lisa isn't here.

The footsteps stop, but I don't hear his door close. I yell again.

"Tyler! Buddy! Are you out there? Are you okay?" The pain notching up with each word.

Still nothing. My throat is hurting from yelling so loud, only slightly distracting me from my arm.

"Tyler. Are you able..." I stop, hearing his footsteps come to the door.

Then silence again. Lisa could walk in at any minute. I have no time to waste.

"Tyler." I yell, though not as loudly now. "Come on in, buddy. It's okay. Daddy needs your help."

The knob on the door turns slowly, and he pushes the door open just enough to squeeze in. He looks worse than ever. His face is so white. He looks ill. His eyes are sunken even more so, as if he's not been sleeping at all. He's staring at me, void of any expression.

"Oh, Tyler. Thank goodness it's you," I say, giving him my most excited smile at his arrival, masking my pain.

He walks over to the bed slowly, deliberately, never taking his eyes off of me.

"Can you help me? I need you to help me get loose from these cables," I tell him, hoping he doesn't question what's going on.

Sitting on the edge of the bed, he faces me. A look of mild curiosity appears on his face.

"Tyler? Can you?" I ask again.

He faces me and smiles. An innocent and sweet smile. I suddenly feel such pity for him. There's a sadness in him that I can't quite reason. I can feel it, but I know he's going to help me. I can feel that too. He sits on the edge of the bed for a few minutes, perhaps torn between betraying his mother and doing what he knows to be right.

Finally, he turns and climbs up onto the bed. Reaching his arms up to the headboard, I notice his nails are long and dirty, like he's been playing in the mud. They look old and chipped. He shifts and starts to climb up over me. The nails on his right hand screech across the headboard with a horrible noise, sending chills down my spine and leaving a scratch in the wood. He sits up on my chest with his legs on either side of me. He smiles, then leans forward and puts his hands on both sides of my head, on the pillow. His face directly above mine. Still smiling, he opens his mouth.

The inside of his mouth is pitch black. There are no teeth, or tongue. Nothing but blackness. He opens it further and now I can see little white dots in there. They are moving. Opening even further, his mouth stretches beyond what any normal human should be able to accomplish. His jaws unhinge, his entire head is opening in half, the gaping hole pointing right at me. In it, the white dots continue to slowly move past the opening. I know what they are. Stars. The inside of his head is like looking into deep space.

I look up above the hole that was his face and see his eyes. They have gone all white.

THEN HE SCREAMS. He no longer even has a mouth, but somehow he still screams.

"YOU. DID. THIS!"

I scream too.

I JOLT awake to the sound of the garage door opening. I'm drenched in sweat. Looking back and forth, there's no one else in the room with me. No sign of Tyler. Images of his half-open head still stuck in my mind. It looked like galaxies inside. Infinite space and time. I shiver at the thought. Lying here now, looking through the slit in the blinds, I can tell it's still dark out. I hear a car door shut and moments later, noises coming from the kitchen. It's Lisa. I expect that she'll come down here to the bedroom to check on me soon. The noise of cabinets closing and dishes clanking stops for a moment, and I hear Tyler. It sounds like he's in his room. He's saying something over and over but I can't tell what it is. An instant fear grips me tight, and I pray that he does not come in here. Even if it was a dream, the vision of his half-open head and mouth filled with an unexplained blackness won't get out of my thoughts.

As expected, Lisa comes down the hall a few minutes later. I try to relax and look normal just as she opens the bedroom door.

"What have you been doing?" The first words out of her mouth.

"I...umm...I've been lying here." I say, not sure how to play this.

"Well, yeah, but you're all sweaty. Are you getting sick?" She walks over and puts her hand on my forehead.

"I don't know, honestly. My throat hurts a little," I say, wondering if this is a good opportunity to fake an illness.

Maybe it will give me a chance to get untied.

"Nope. No fever. "I bet you just need some more rest. I'm surprised you are awake at this hour," she mentions, and with no clear concept of time I have to take her at her word.

"What time is it? I thought I just heard Tyler up. He's singing or something," I say.

"It's late." She mentions, not giving me any more information than that, and ignoring my comment about Tyler.

Touching my face to again assess my physical condition, she comments "You're fine. You just need to relax. Maybe a movie or something?"

She grabs the remote and fumbles with it before dropping it at her feet. As she shuffles to bend down and get it, I hear her accidentally kick it under the bed.

"Well, now I'm the butterfingers," she says while getting down beside the bed to retrieve the controller.

Just as she disappears from my view, I remember the twist tie, sending my heart racing.

"Ugh. I don't think I can reach the damn thing," she huffs. "Wait...got it. I really need to clean under here."

She starts to stand back up, remote in hand, allowing my pounding heart a reprieve.

"Okay, what are you in the mood for? A western? You love westerns," she asks.

"Umm. Yes, actually. That would be..."

She interrupts me, looking down at her feet. "Wait... what the...?" She leans back down by the bed, and I know that's all over for me now.

"Oh, you little liar." She speaks calmly, standing up with the twist tie in her other hand.

"Babe, I... Listen... I..." I begin.

"Babe? Don't fucking babe me now. You little fucking liar." The calmness in her voice scaring me worse than if she were yelling. "Oh, you cannot be trusted. So, so cannot be trusted."

"I wasn't going anywhere. I wasn't going to leave my family. I was going to be sitting right here when you got back, to show you that I want to stay, even if I could leave." My lie sounding almost convincing to my own ears.

"Deception is not the path to trust." She jabs, and I bite back the urge to point out how much deception she has played since I first woke up in the hospital.

It wouldn't do any good. She's crazy and irrational.

"You know, Steve, I'm not sure you're ever getting out of this bed, because you simply cannot be trusted." She seems like she's almost talking to herself out loud now. "I have just the cure for you."

She drops the remote on my chest with a thud, then turns on her heel to the door. Twist tie still in her other hand, she walks out, shutting the door behind her. The moment the door shuts, I know what her plan is. She's going to drug me again so that I sleep, maybe even overdose. I pull my right arm hard on the restraints for a moment. There's simply no escaping this. I am going to die. Pulling hard on my arm restraint once more, the pain in my body coming back to life, I notice it. The black plastic tubing on the outside of the cables has slid downward near my right wrist. Straining my neck to get a better look, I see that the cables aren't really cables at all. They are little chains covered by the black tubing. The chain connects to a link on the handcuff with a little clamp. The clamp is fastened by a threaded screw. But it's loose, exposing the open clamp. If I could get a little slack on the chain, I might be able to unhook the handcuff from it. I've only got a few moments before Lisa comes back in here and drugs me again.

Taking a quick, deep breath, I pull my left arm out of the sling. The pain instantly springs to life. It feels like a giant bruise that I keep poking at. Another deep breath and I reach up and over my body, trying to pull the black plastic tubing down a little more near my wrist. Spikes of raw pain shoot from my shoulder to my finger. I'm sweating worse and my hand is slippery again. Grabbing the clamp with my index finger, I pull. My arm is suddenly afire with pain when the handcuff chain pops loose from the cable and my right arm is free. For a moment, I can't register that it was that easy. I have no time to think, and I sit upright on the bed. Dots appear in front of my face for a moment and I feel a little dizzy. How long have I been tied down like this? I can't recall and it doesn't matter. I have to hurry. Pushing my left arm back into the sling subsides the pain a little, but not completely. Using my now-freed right hand, I lean forward and slide the plastic tubing up near my ankles. My legs are connected to the chains with the same screw clamps, but these aren't loose. Twisting the threaded connectors proves to be easy and my legs are free moments later. Pulling both legs off the bed, I stand, anticipating another wave of dizziness. It doesn't come, but my legs are shaky, finally being in use again has them quivering as normal blood circulation starts returning. I limp to the bedroom door and lock it from the inside. Turning back around, I notice the scratch on the headboard from Tyler's nails. Before I have time to process how that could possibly be, I scan the room for any kind of weapon. Lisa will be here any moment and I have no plan. I see nothing and there's no time to search. For all I know, Lisa has a gun. I look to the bedroom window. It's my only chance. I walk over to the window, feeling some of the strength and steadiness return to my legs. Upon unlocking and opening the window, I notice that it's up a little higher than I expected. Ground level outside the house is lower than the flooring in this room, so I'm going to have a little bit of a drop. Pushing the screen out, I reach out with my good arm and pull myself up. My left arm dragging against the windowsill in a spike of pain. I bang my head on the window frame getting it through the opening. It hurts, and it's loud. I suddenly hear the doorknob turn behind me. It starts to twist frantically. I'm almost through the window when I hear what sounds like glass shattering out in the hall.

"What the fuck are you doing? Steve! Open the door! Open this fucking door NOW!" Lisa screams through the door.

I'm almost through the window when I realize there's nothing for me to grab onto on the outside of the house. No way for me to balance and pull my legs out in front of me. Lisa is pounding on the door. I hear wood splintering behind me.

Pulling myself out to my torso, I attempt to wedge myself

sideways in the window opening to pull one of my legs through, but it's no use. My right hand slips and I fall, face first. I try to roll forward but instead land on my back and shoulders, directly on top of the shrubs. Limbs pierce my skin and shirt, sending a burning pain all along my neck and shoulders. For a moment, the banging on the door stops and I'm lying here in silence. Then, I hear an explosion of shattering wood. Lisa is in the bedroom, her voice getting closer. Almost on top of me now.

"What are you...? " She walks up to the window, looking down at me.

"You...You MOTHERFUCKER! Oh...you just wait. You liar! LIAR! Liar...liar.." She turns away and disappears from view. I hear her voice fading deeper into the house. She's heading toward the front door. Getting up as fast as I can, pain shooting through my left hand and shoulder, I run full force across the front yard. Looking back, I see the house. The garage door is still open. Lisa's car parked in it. It's a white Mercedes. As soon as I see it, it sends a cold fear down to my stomach. I get a flash in my mind of Lisa driving this car. The airbag going off in her face.

Running out into the road in front of the house, I scan for a car or a person or anyone I can flag down. I look back at the house again. She hasn't come out. I run across the street to the front door of the neighbor's house and pound on it as hard as I can.

"Help me! I'm being attacked!" I scream.

I see lights in the living room, but no one answers the door. I run to the next house, my throat raw from screaming, my arm burning with pain. Almost to the door, I trip over a low garden fence, twisting my ankle and landing on my bad arm. The pain is like white hot fire in my bones. Straining to get up, I feel my ankle throbbing. Chancing yet another look back, there is still no sign of Lisa. Just as I'm turning away, I catch a glimpse of something from the corner of my eye. I look back yet again and see the front door fly open. Lisa comes running out. She's got a wooden ax held high above her head. Her face, a murderous rage. I turn and run as fast as I can. My ankle and my arm fighting for attention. My freedom and my safety paramount.

Quickly scanning the next few houses on both sides of the road, I see that they all have tall fences with gates. I have nowhere to hide. Running along the edge of the road, hobbling on my ankle, I'm screaming over and over again, as loud as I can. I don't even know what I'm saying and it doesn't matter. Someone must hear me. Someone will come outside to help. My lungs are burning through my chest. My ankle fighting to steal some of the pain from my arm. I feel something sticky and wet on the back of my neck and my back. Blood from the fall into the shrubs. I look back quickly to see Lisa again. Even with the ax held high, she's gaining on me. Running past the entrance to the neighborhood, I have no idea of where to go. Then I remember the brick wall. The rope. If I can make it through the woods in the dark, maybe I can climb the rope.

Just as I feel like I can't run anymore, I push harder and pick up speed. My twisted ankle giving a stabbing jolt with each step. I can hear her footsteps now. She is closing in on me. I make the last turn on the edge of the road, then cut across into the woods. It's almost pitch black. I'm running full speed and can't see a thing. Branches from the trees scrape across my face. A twig catches my sling and rips loose the shoulder strap. My arm is suddenly ablaze with new pain, the sling flying off into the darkness. The pain is unbearable. I have to stop. Making a sharp right turn, I slide down on my knees behind a bush and grab my bad arm with my good one. In the distance, I hear a dog barking, but no sign of Lisa. I strain to listen for her footsteps but hear nothing. Aside from the dog, the neighborhood is strangely devoid of any noises. No voices or cars. Looking down at my arms, I feel my last bit of energy dissolve. I simply can't go any further. My arm is a mass of fiery pain. My hand is sending little spikes of raw pain to my fingertips. The muscles in my legs throbbing and fluttering into knots, and my ankle is now a dull ache. Closing my eyes, I need to rest. To sleep. Just for a minute. Let her find me. It doesn't matter now. Opening my eyes, I see the streetlight out by the road. Directly below it and just off the road, I see footprints in the dirt. I can tell they aren't Lisa's because I recognize them. They are just like the ones from before. They look like prints from a man's dress shoe. How can they still be here?

As if in answer to my thought, I see him. My father.

Here in the dark of night, his face is as clear as day. Exactly like I remember it. He hasn't aged a day. He's wearing a suit and carrying a purple Mylar balloon. It has writing on it, but I can't tell what it says here in the dark. Walking through the wooded space between the streetlight and where I'm hiding, he stops in front of me and leans down.

"Oh, son, this isn't for you. It's not time yet." He pauses. "You have to pull it together. They still need you."

He extends an open hand. I reach up to grab it, expecting my hand to go through his, like a ghost. But his hand is solid and he grabs tight, pulling me up on my feet. My pain momentarily vanished. I feel a stream of tears running down my face.

"I have so many questions, Dad. How are you here? Who needs me? Lisa? Tyler? I'm going insane. Tyler is a monster. Lisa is crazy. Who is Haley?" I ask, all at once.

"Focus on the things that matter right now. What matters is your life. Take it back. It's not this woman's life. It is yours."

"What is this? I don't understand. Why can't you just tell me what's going on?" I plead with him.

"I have done everything I can. I tried to tell you, son. Tried to remind you, but there's only so much I can do." He speaks in riddles, like Haley and my Mom.

He stands up and lets go of the balloon. As it passes up into the lower branches of the trees above, he says, "Reach for what you feel, and forget about what does and does not make sense. Things are not what they seem. That woman is a witch. I'm not the one in control of this, but you can't waste anymore time. You have to go now or not at all," he says, then smiles at me.

My fear of Lisa catching me is gone. Deep down inside, I feel a sudden clarity. I know that, if I just need to listen to what he is telling me, everything will be okay. It doesn't make any rational sense, but it's true. But I'm confused by the vagueness of his words. Just as I start to ask him to clarify, he winks and then disappears into nothing. Just like that.

The pain instantly returns to my body, and I'm left lost in the woods. Alone.

With no idea of how to proceed, I yell in desperation. "Go where?!"

My voice echoes off of the trees. All at once, I hear something crashing through the woods, coming right for me.

It's her.

I've given away my position.

As fast as I can, I get my bearings and move toward the back of the woods, heading for the wall. My ankle, my arm, my finger, and my back are all in unison. A choir of screaming pain. I feel my energy leaving me again, but I'm almost to the wall.

It's so dark back here. Almost pitch black. I can't see anything. I have no choice but to slow down. Walking now, I can't hear anything behind me and I wonder for a moment if I actually lost her in this darkness. I slow to a stop and turn back around to listen behind me. The night is silent again. For a moment, I think I hear the rustling of leaves. Listening intently, I can't hear anything over the pounding of my own heart.

. . .

THEN, I hear her breathing.

Right in my ear.

I BREAK into a run just as I hear her voice, inches from my face.

"NOOO!" Her throat sounds wet and full of phlegm.

I run blindly for the wall, smacking right into her. We both go down in a tumble. My body is only pain. There is nothing else. Rolling back to my knees, I immediately stand and run. She is right behind me.

"You fucking liar!" Her breath on the back of my neck. "I'm going to kill you. I'm going to make it hurt, like you did to my boy."

I don't know how, but I'm starting to put distance between us. Her voice is getting farther away.

"My poor, sweet boy. I know what you did!" Her voice even farther behind me now. "You and your slut. You took him from me! I saw you! You know I saw you!"

Grabbing the rope with both hands, I feel something deep inside my right shoulder tear and pop loose. My fingers on my left hand clicking and grinding. The pain is blinding. Pulling myself up, wrestling with the knotted rope, it feels impossible to climb. Hand over hand, I'm almost to the top when I feel the rope go tight.

She's climbing it underneath me.

Her weight steadies the rope, making it easier to climb. My left arm and hand are a mass of raw nerves. I'm at the top of the wall. It feels higher than I thought. Maybe ten feet. I wrangle my right leg up and over, straddling the wall. The top is made of wide flat brick. Briefly looking to the other side, I see that the sun is coming up. The ground on the other side slopes up and out to a peak. Like a small mountain. It's all grey and black soil, like a construction site that caught on fire. Pieces of debris jutting up out of the ground. Broken sticks of timber and iron piping poking up here and there.

With the new light of the sunrise, I chance looking down the rope I just climbed. Just barely, but I see her. She's almost on me, a dark moving shape on the rope. I lean forward on my arms and pull my left leg up and over. My left arm buckles under my own weight, blasting new pain into my body and causing me to lie forward onto my chest for a moment. Sitting back up, both legs hanging over the construction site side of the wall, I panic for a moment, unable to find the rope on this side.

There it is. I use my good hand to grab on, adjusting my legs to find the rope knots on this side.

But it's too late. She's here. On the top of the wall with me. I see the faint outline of the ax above her head. I hear it cutting through the air for a split second. Releasing my grip on the rope, I slide down a notch. Not far enough. The ax comes down hard. The blade missing my arm by inches, it slams into the wall between my inner arm and my ribs. The wooden handle making contact with my left arm. I hear the wet sound of my skin splitting open. The crunch of bones shattering. My mind is emptied of everything but the intense pain that has blinded me to everything else around me. I feel my bladder release, hot urine running down my legs. My grip on the rope is lost, my head scraping along the wall on the way down. I feel blood running down my face and into my eyes. Landing on my twisted ankle, it brings the pain away from my arm for an instant, but no more. I land in a heap.

The ground is soft and cool. I want to stay here forever and never move again. Anything to escape the pain. Anything. But then I hear the ax scraping along the wall. She's climbing down above me. Closer. Closer. With my last bit of strength, I roll over and sit up. The morning sun's light illuminating the wall. She's almost down. Her face masked by her hair, but I can see still see it.

She's smiling.

GETTING TO MY FEET, I try to run but it's no use. My ankle is broken. Every step is a new explosion of pain. My left arm is a stranger, flopping around like extra weight. I stagger up the peak, shouting for help.

"PLEASE, HELP ME! ANYONE! HELP ME!" My voice cracking. My throat raw. A mix of tears and blood in my mouth.

I'm almost to the top of the peak. Turning back, I see Lisa drop from the last foot of the rope to her feet. She immediately breaks into a full sprint towards me.

At the top of the hill, I look down the other side. A giant chasm spans at least fifty feet across. It must be two hundred feet deep. The rising sun gives me glimpses of the bottom. Piles of broken asphalt. It's a dead end. Looking back, Lisa is almost on me. Still in a full sprint, she is quickly closing the gap between us. I chance inching up the very edge of the cliff and look down. Straight down. There's no path. No ladder. No rope. The drop looks bottomless at first, making me dizzy. Broken beams and sheets of metal sticking out from the walls of the chasm all the way down.

I look back to Lisa. She is right here, only a few feet from me, still coming at full speed. The ax above her head. I duck at the last minute and push myself toward her legs. Tripping over my back, she drops the ax over the cliff. Like a cat, she spins in midair and grabs my left arm. I hear a howl of pain before I realize it's my own voice. Her momentum carries her over the edge, dragging me along with her.

We are both in the air. It's almost peaceful. She lets go of my arm. Her hair blowing straight up from the fall, I see her face. The terror gone. For a moment there's a beauty in her face, and I suddenly feel a great swell of sadness for her. Then, she smiles. A big sinister smile. She reaches for my arm again. In an instant, I hear the thud of her landing on something...and then she's gone.

Frantically grabbing at the air with my good arm, I feel my other arm flapping lifeless in the wind. The jagged ends of a dozen broken beams poking out at me like giant fingers of an ancient robot, just out of reach. Suddenly, the sleeve of my shirt catches onto the tip of one of the beams as it digs deep into my good arm. I can barely feel it. The fabric of my shirt makes a ripping sound so loud it startles me. Suddenly, I stop falling, hanging there by the shoulder of my shirt, I feel a fresh stream of hot blood rolling down my arm. It drips off of my fingertips. Down, down into the black abyss. I can barely see the bottom. A wave of lightheadedness comes over me, and I know I've lost too much blood. I look back up and see her. Peeking over the edge of a metal shelf, sticking out of the cliff wall. Her smile widens.

"You could have stayed with us. We could have been happy. She leans out farther, her voice strangely calm again. "But you chose this instead. You'll pay. One way or another, you will pay."

As if by some unseen force, right on queue, the metal plate she's on starts to bend. Before she has time to retreat from the edge, it folds in half, dropping her straight down. I feel the wind of her body whiz past me, her hair all in her face. Reaching up with my good arm, I test the stability of the beam I'm hanging from. It responds with a loud snap and I join Lisa again in falling. Farther this time. Faster and faster. Down below me, maybe thirty feet, I see her falling. Her back is facing the ground, her face staring straight up at me. She raises her arms toward me.

"Noooooo!!!" she screams.

Looking past her, I see the chunks of old broken concrete

coming up to meet us at blinding speed, their dark cracks like menacing smiles waiting to open and swallow me whole. I close my eyes. My heart is slamming through my chest. This is it. This is the end. I'll never see Haley now. I'll never be able to tell her what happened. To tell her why I couldn't find her. Why I couldn't remember her. I couldn't remember us. I couldn't remember my life with her.

I couldn't remember...

...BUT THEN, I do.

I do remember.

I remember...everything.

———————

26

Haley knows I'm not very good at surprises, so I'm doing my best to feign ignorance here.

"Looks like a pretty mellow weekend coming up, which will be nice." I say. "Work has been crazy busy for me this week."

Business has been insanely busy, as of late. My firm has a new contract with a major building developer and we've been designing their electrical systems day and night. Haley looks over at me and smiles that crooked little smile that I know so well. She's beautiful, and I'm distracted by that for a moment before she replies.

"Same here. We've taken on more new clients this week than we have in the entire last month. A weekend of relaxation would be nice," she replies.

She recently made junior Vice President of Marketing, and her work has been really taking a lot of her time lately too, but her response still makes me wonder if she's on to my little game here.

Eight years. It feels like so much less time, and somehow so much more. A couple of months ago, I told her that—for once—

I wanted to make the plans for our anniversary. Openly and pleasantly surprised by this, she'd agreed. She's always been the one to organize and set up these things. This time, it's on me.

She deserves it. I haven't said a word about it since then, with the idea that she'll think I forgot. I'm hoping to blow her away with this one. If she's on to me, she's probably thinking I made dinner plans at a nice restaurant, maybe even a movie or the theater. I can't wait to see her reaction when she finds out I've actually booked a three-day weekend at a great hotel in Florida. Right on the beach. All expenses paid. Three days isn't much for such a long trip, but neither of us can afford to be away from our jobs for much longer right now. Even so, I'm so excited I can hardly hide it.

We're driving home from the downtown marketplace. We've spent almost four hours of walking from shop to shop, weaving among the never ending crowds of locals. It's been an enjoyable day with her, but I'm so ready for a quiet night at home. Maybe we'll grill steaks and pair up a nice wine.

Traffic is always bad leaving the marketplace, but we lucked out today and missed it. As we approach the light, I consider which direction to go. Haley picked me up from the office earlier today, and we should go back there and get my truck, but it's Friday. It can wait. We've got all weekend to get my truck, and I want to take the back way back home. Besides, as much as I won't admit it aloud, her car is much more fun to drive. I turn right at the light and punch the gas for a second, just to get her attention.

She looks over at me and smiles, then leans forward and turns up the radio. "Hey, Speed Racer, you're going to get a ticket."

Just then, "Waves" comes on. It's a cheesy pop song about teenage romance, but we both love it, and I usually sing the chorus because I'm terrible singer and it makes her laugh. The music jumps right into a heavy piano piece, with rock drums in between.

"Honey, it's you and me..." the song starts, and cheesy or not, it fits the mood perfectly.

I regain normal speed and take in the fresh air. Slowing down for the turn, we exit the main road and start the route back on Acorn Street. It twists around three different lakes, and it's full of hills. It's beautiful. Driving on this road always make me feel like I'm in a car commercial. More so now since our car is still new. Technically, it's her car. I get car sick when someone else is driving, so she let's me drive it. It's a black convertible Mini Cooper. It was a little more than we wanted to spend, but as hard and often as she works, she deserves that too. Not an overly manly car, and not what I would have chosen for myself, but at least she's not the type to put girly bumper stickers on it, or line the dash with stuffed animals. Aside from the little dream catcher that I bought her hanging from the rearview mirror, it could be my car.

We drive in silence for a minute or so, enjoying the sunshine.

"This is wonderful, just what we need," I say aloud, before I realize how sappy that sounds. This isn't something I'd normally say, and I'm ready for her to tease me about sounding like a Hallmark card. She doesn't. Instead, she turns down the radio a few notches, then reaches over and squeezes my hand.

"You are Mr. Wonderful," she says.

"I'll remember you said that." I say. I use a hint of sarcasm, but I still mean it. Now I'll be the one to tease her for sounding like a greeting card. A small giggle escapes her lips. I look over for a moment and take a look at her. She's got her shoes off with her bare feet on the dash. Her toenails are painted an unusual shade of blue. That color reminds me of the shade of a snow cone I bought once at the county fair that tasted even better than it looked. She catches me looking at her and does a kissy face, as if to tease me in an entirely different way.

I look back at the road just in time to see a faded white van backing out right in front of us, the words 'Living Color Painting' running along its side. The driver turns towards me, a young woman with a crazy pile of curly red hair piled on top of her head. Hitting the brakes full force and swerving hard to the right to avoid hitting her, I feel Haley's head bump my shoulder as she's thrown into me, her hands fly up in front of her, rolling the radio knob up full blast. Her hair slapping across my face, the cab fills with blaring music. We miss the van by inches but now I'm straddling the road. The front tires losing their traction, we start sliding sideways off the edge of the road. The radio singing "...whenever we touch..." fills my ears. The right rear end of the car smacks hard into a bright red mailbox, snapping it off and throwing us into a flat spin. I've lost all control of the car and hold tight to the steering wheel as hard as I can. We continue sliding and spinning, sliding and spinning. Then, I feel us slowing down. Song lyrics still blasting in the car, "It's electric, this thing we got." We finally stop spinning. I press harder on the brakes as we come to a full stop in the opposite lane, directly facing the bottom of a hill. I chance a look over to see if Haley is okay. She's frozen, looking at the road in front of us, her face a mask of terror. I follow her gaze. From over the hill in front us, a white Mercedes comes barreling down. It must be going twice the speed limit, yet everything switches to slow motion right before it hits us head-on. A blonde woman is driving. They are so close; I can see that her eyes are a stunning grayish blue. A young boy sits in the passenger seat. A green pine tree air freshener hangs from their rearview mirror. As we make contact, their faces are suddenly hidden by their airbags. The radio, oblivious to the trauma unfolding, continues "I'm so happy to have found you." Sudden spurts of a red liquid hit the roof right above where the boy's face was a moment ago. A cardboard box flies up out of their backseat, and a swarm of plastic bottle caps makes their way through the bursting windshield in a spray of colors. My airbag goes off, punching me in the nose and pushing Haley's dream catcher up into the air. The song blares "Girl, it's you and me, like the waves upon the sea." I feel the feathers on it tickling my forehead for just an instant.

THE NOISE IS SO sudden and so loud.

THEN, nothing.
    Black. Silent.

I'M IN A HOSPITAL. I can hear the nurse call station paging Dr. June Goodall. The intercom voice raspy, yet high pitched. I'm being wheeled down a hall on a gurney. I can't open my eyes. I can't move. But I can feel the wheels clicking along the linoleum floor.

Tick-tock. Tick-tock. Tick-tock. Haley is here. She's holding my hand.

"I love you," she tells me.

I try to speak but nothing comes out.

I want to say it back before I die. Just please let me say it back once.

I try again. Nothing. I'm fading. I'm falling. Falling down inside my own head.

THEN, nothing.
    Black. Silent.

.   .   .

I'M STILL in the hospital. In a room now. It's quieter. Haley is still with me. I can't see her, but I smell her jasmine perfume. I can't wake up. I try with all of my mind to wake up, to move my body. I can't. She's holding my hand again. I can't even hold hers back.

"I love you, Steve. Don't leave me. Stay with me."

I will. I promise in my head. I will.

THEN, nothing.

Black. Silent.

I HEAR HER VOICE. She's talking to someone else. She is yelling.

"Just be honest with me. That's all I'm asking. It's been three fucking weeks and I can't get a straight answer from any of you people!"

I've never heard her this angry before in my life. I hear someone walking close to me. I'm lying down. Still in a bed.

"Mrs. Lewis, I know that this is a very difficult time, but we are doing everything that we can. The doctor will be back in later tonight to review the latest results of testing." It's an older woman's voice. The nurse.

"More words without actually saying anything. Is my husband going to die? Is he going to wake up? Is he going to be stuck in this coma forever?" She sounds frantic.

"These are things we simply don't know yet, Mrs. Lewis... Haley. I'm so sorry. I wish I knew more." The nurse's voice becoming soft and soothing.

"I know...I'm sorry." Haley's voice drops into a whisper. "I... I'm just so scared. I need to know what to expect is all." She is crying now. I can hear it.

"Haley, I'm not supposed to say anything that we don't know for sure. But, if I might say something off the record?" She glances over her shoulder, to make sure no one is within earshot. "I want you to prepare yourself. It doesn't look promising." The nurse's words echo in my head. "promising...promising...promising."

Her voice fades. Further and further away, like I'm falling back into myself again.

FALLING. Endlessly falling.

All around me, black. Darkness. Silent.

My stomach is in my throat.

FAR BELOW, I see something. A pinprick of light.

I'm falling toward it.

My eyes are open.

My eyes are closed.

I CAN SEE the backs of my eyelids. Red splotches dance around in front of me. It's quiet. I can hear the whir of some machine nearby. I can feel the IV in my arm. I can smell her perfume again. I hear her breathing nearby. I'm still falling. In the hall outside the room, I hear the footsteps of visitors, doctors and nurses walking by. They never seem to stop.

Falling. An overhead tone beeps through the intercom.

AM I HERE, or am I somewhere else? Am I dreaming? Am I home?

. . .

FALLING.

The light below me grows larger, now the size of a manhole. Falling. Closer.

ONE SET of footsteps starts getting closer. The nurse coming into my room again.

"Did you try the tacos downstairs? They are amazing." The nurse's voice. Playful.

"I've been eating here for a while now," Haley tells her. "Why do I feel like you're lying?" She questions the nurse.

"Because I am," the nurse says, and they both laugh. She's happy for a moment, and that makes me happy.

MAYBE SHE'S STARTING to let go. Maybe she should. I'm trapped like this. Maybe forever. I push with everything I am to try and speak. To move. Nothing.

THE LIGHT IS big enough to drive a car through.

I'm closer and closer, falling into the light

HALEY? My wife? Lisa? Is Lisa my wife? Am I sleeping? Am I dreaming? In my house, is someone there...in the hallway?

I HEAR the nurse's footsteps walk right up to me. Her cold hand on my face. I hear her clicking a pen...No, a flashlight. The dark red behind my eyelids changes to a lighter red. I feel her hand on my eyelid. She pulls open my right eye. I can see her! She looks old. Her face a mass of wrinkles. She smiles and all of her teeth are yellow and crooked.

"How are we doing today, Steve-O?" she says.

She shines the flashlight into my right eye. It's blinding but I can't close my eye. I try to call out.

"Hey!" My own voice startling me.

The nurse lets go of my eyelid, dropping the light.

Haley's voice. "Oh my God! Hey! You can hear me?!"

I try to reply again but can't.

FALLING.

Time to let go.

I FALL through the light into...nothing.

Nothing.

Black. Darkness.

The noise is so sudden and so loud, I jerk awake with a jolt. Sitting upright. Looking around. That hospital room. The flowers in the vases. The cards with no names. The TV is on but with no sound. A car commercial is on. A black convertible sports car whizzes down a hilly country road. Haley's car. The road to our house. On the far wall, a purple Mylar balloon is scraping back and forth, making a little crinkly sound. It has words printed on it. I strain to focus on them. *'Wake up. This isn't real.'* printed neatly in bold white letters. My left hand is wrapped up in a cast from the middle of my forearm. A bandage on my forehead.

Lisa is there, wearing her white Mercedes t-shirt. She is sleeping. With each breath, her shirt turns black, then back to white, then back to black. She is really sleeping. But how can that be? This is all in my head. This isn't real, is it?

I do remember.
I remember everything.

I OPEN MY EYES AGAIN. I'm still falling in the construction site.

Lisa is falling below me. For a moment I wonder what happened to the ax.

It doesn't matter now. Nothing matters now.

THE BROKEN CONCRETE below is so close now. So close. I see it rushing up behind Lisa. Sixty feet. Fifty. Forty. I don't want to see this. I close my eyes. Lisa makes a sudden, guttural moaning sound, forcing me to look. Just as I see her slam into a jutting piece of concrete, her back arching backwards, blood sprays from her face.

Instantly, she comes rushing back up towards me, her face stretching open into a mass of impossibly long and pointy teeth.

· · ·

I CLOSE MY EYES.

29

I open my eyes.

I SEE nothing but blurriness for a minute. Slowly, my eyes adjust and I see that I'm in a hospital room. There's a commotion out in the hall. I hear the voices of people yelling as a group of nurses run past my room, a doctor running behind them, trying to catch up. Now I can hear them in the room adjacent to mine, yelling.

"We're losing her! I need those paddles!" I hear a man yelling.

"Almost here, doctor." A woman's voice.

"Why weren't they already in here?!" The man again.

Now the voices are all on top of each other and I am struggling to understand them. A man runs by my door with some type of equipment in his arms. More commotion from the other room. A few minutes go by and the noise dies down.

Oh, please, not again. Is this a dream within a dream

...within a dream? My head starts to hurt. Looking around, I see that my arm is still in a cast. I sit up, and instantly feel my body groan with aches and pains all over. I feel so weak. I carefully scan the room. No balloons, no cards, and the TV is off. There is no one in the room with me or any sign that anyone has recently been here. Wait, that's not true. I see a coffee cup sitting on the counter near the sink. It's from Enzo's. Her favorite coffee there was Turkish coffee, black and thick, with a pinch of salt. It was so gross but Haley loved it. Loves it. My wife, Haley. I remember.

I REMEMBER EVERYTHING.

THE ACCIDENT.
The Mercedes.
The lady and her son. I remember their faces.
Lisa and Tyler.

A CHILL RUNS OVER ME. They were just strangers.
My thoughts are interrupted when a woman walks into my room with a tray of donuts.

HALEY.

SHE'S WEARING panda pajama bottoms and a plain white t-shirt and she's beautiful. Tears fill my eyes before I speak.
"Hello, Mrs. Wonderful" I say. My voice, a scruffy whisper.
She drops the donuts. They land in a little pile, one rolling unceremoniously back out the door.

"OH MY GOD! OH MY GOD! YOU'RE AWAKE! YOU'RE..." She runs over to me so quickly that I'm half afraid she's going to plow me over.

My face in her hands. Her lips touch mine. I smell her perfume, it's jasmine. Feel her tears on my face. I reach up and put my good arm around her.

"Steve. Oh, Steve...I...Oh my God. I've missed you. I've missed you so much." She breaks into loud sobs.

"I know. I missed you too." I say, and I mean it.

WE SPEND the next few hours talking. I've been in a coma for almost six weeks. Haley has been here every day. Her business has suffered. My business has suffered, but we will survive. My skull was fractured during the accident and my arm was broken. The fracture is healing as expected, and although I have to take it easy for a while, the doctor expects I'll make a full recovery. I have had no surgery on my brain, and the realism of the dream I've been having hits me, making me feel almost as if the dream surgery was a mechanism for me to forget more of my real life. That idea being ludicrous, of course, yet it still lingers in my head.

My arm was a clean break, and no shoulder or finger damage. They expect it will heal fine too. I raise it up as high as I can to test the pain, and find that it doesn't hurt to lift. As I'm comforted by that fact, I look again at my cast and notice writing on it. In blue pen, it says, "COME BACK TO ME" in perfectly scribed letters, alongside a hand drawn heart. Haley sees me looking at it.

"I know, it's corny. But it apparently worked," she smiles.

"Indeed, it did," I reply.

Looking at her now, I remember everything about her, about my house, my dog, my business, my life. So much of it was in my dream. Danny had really been here. He spoke to me while I slept and I heard him. I remember him too.

Then, it dawns on me. My mom was. I know this, yet I ask anyway.

"Was my mom here?" I ask Haley.

"Yes! She was! You heard her!"

"I did. I...I wondered why she kept asking me if I could hear her," I say.

"Oh my God, you did hear her. Steve, she's old and set in her ways, but she does love you. She really does." She reminds me, and her face is so earnest, like she just wants everything to be okay with everyone now. She's beautiful. I remember her face. The little scar on her chin. I remember her talking to me. Constantly talking to me. Telling me not to be scared. Telling me that everything would be ok. Telling me she loves me.

"I know she does. I know." I say.

"My dad...was...I mean.." I trail off, not sure what I was going to ask. My father is gone. I know this.

"Your dad?" Haley asks, looking confused. "Steve, you do remember that your dad is...?"

"Yes, yes. Of course. I guess I...I had such a vivid dream. My mom was there, you were there and he was there too. In a way, I think he was..." My voice drops down to a low whisper.

"Oh, babe. I'm sorry. So sorry." Haley interrupts my thoughts.

I consider telling her about my dad and about Lisa and Tyler but don't. I'm not sure why. I guess it all seems irrelevant now.

"Is my doctor's name Lambert, by chance? Or Bowen" I ask, feeling as if I know the answer before she tells me.

"No. You've mostly been seen by Doctor Pearson. Why?" she asks.

"Ahh...never mind. Just more silly dreams, I guess." I reply, wondering where I got those names in my head. Perhaps from the running television? I'm starting to get a gnawing feeling that some of the things from my dream were planted in my head by design. Knowing how silly that sounds, I try to brush it off.

THE NURSES and doctors come and go. They take blood samples and my temperature for what seems like the tenth time. Haley introduces me to Gladys. She is an older nurse with shoulder length, white hair, a million wrinkles on her face, and a mouth full of crooked, yellow teeth. She's the head nurse who's been assigned to me, and aside from her appearance, she seems very sweet and warm.

"Nice to meet you, Gladys," I say.

"Oh, we've met Steve-O, but it's been a bit of a one-sided relationship." She jokes.

"Well, for what it's worth, even though we've never spoken, I do appreciate it." I say.

"Oh, we've spoken too, but I think you talk in your sleep." She smiles at Haley. "That's how you know when he's not telling the truth, huh?"

Haley smiles back. "Oh, you know it. I can't tell you how many times he's cheated on dieting and told me in his sleep."

They both share a laugh.

"Wait!" I say. "I've been talking this whole time?"

"No, no. We're just teasing you. You only spoke twice. First time was a few weeks back. I was checking your pupils and you yelled, 'Hey!' Frankly, you scared the heck out of both of us." Gladys chuckles. Haley and her exchange smiles.

"You spoke again only three days ago." She smiles at Haley again.

Haley starts to cry again. "I wasn't here the second time, but she told me about it. I never gave up on you, babe, but that did give me a renewed sense of hope." Haley starts to cry again.

Gladys gives Haley a long hug and then looks back at me.

"I was checking your pulse and you started to speak. I'll be honest, as first it wasn't looking promising but after you started becoming responsive...Well, I had a good feeling about things after that." Her grin is friendly and contagious.

She leaves my room and goes on to check other patients. She and the other hospital staff have been working hard to make sure I'm okay to leave. We've asked them to hurry with any tests and procedures so we can go home as soon as possible. I think about home, about that house, and I wonder for a second if my dreams will still haunt me there, but I know they won't. I felt it all wash off of me the moment I woke up. I remember my dog. Annie...Wait, not...not Annie. Artie. He is a boy dog, and the fog between my dreams and reality seems to pull even further away.

IT TAKES three more days for the doctors to give me the go-ahead to leave. I'm almost afraid to sleep each night, afraid I'll return to that dream world. Afraid of Lisa and Tyler. But each night, I do sleep. Perfect, restful, dreamless sleep. During these three days, Haley tells me about the accident. It was really bad and her car is totaled. I'll never get to drive that black Mini Cooper convertible again. Officially, the woman driving the Mercedes was at fault. Although the wreck seemed like it was totally my fault, she was going more than double the speed limit. Haley says there is still an investigation going on, but she's been too preoccupied with my condition to return all the phone calls about it.

WE'RE all packed up and ready and even though I'm feeling like I'm mostly caught up, Haley and I continue to talk for hours at a time. I've missed her so much. We are enjoying each other's company, but we're keeping an eye on the door. We we finally get the all-clear to head home, it can't come soon enough.

"Okay, Mr. and Mrs. Lewis, you are free to go. Now get out of here!" Gladys walks in and says with a smile. That yellow, crooked tooth smile. She helps me into a wheelchair, then wheels me out to the hall and down to the elevator.

Haley calls out, looking back at the other hospital staff. "I would say that I'll miss this place, but that would be a lie. I will miss you guys though!"

"Come by and see us sometime, sweetie," Gladys replies, pushing me along.

"I will do just that! Maybe bring you guys some better food." They both laugh.

As we roll past each room, I glance in and see different people lying in bed. Some have hoses hooked to them. Some look perfectly healthy while others look old and close to death.

"What happened to the woman and her son? The car that crashed into us?" I ask, remembering no one has mentioned the outcome of the passengers in the Mercedes.

"That's such a strange and sad story, I'm afraid." Gladys tells me, her voice dropping low. "The boy died on impact. There's an ongoing investigation around that." She looks at Haley. "I would have thought someone would have contacted you about that by now."

As we board the elevator, Haley speaks.

"It's such a tragedy." Haley says. "I've spoken to the police a couple of times. An insurance agent once. They've left other messages. I just haven't made time to call back."

"Well..." Gladys continues. "We couldn't find any next of kin to notify about the boy. We couldn't really find much information about the woman either, not that I could tell you any of it if we did. It was quite the mystery. We have their names and address, but that's about it. No school or work history. No family and no friends anywhere."

"What the police found in the wreckage of her car was the strangest part," she says.

"Wait." I interrupt, chills threatening to form on my arms. "Did it include plastic bottle caps?"

"Yes!" she proclaims. "Oh my...you remember that?"

"I do. I remember seeing them during the accident," I reply.

"That's crazy that you remember that!" Haley says. "I can't remember much after leaving the marketplace."

"Well, yes, the inside of the cab was full of art supplies. We all assumed they belonged to her son." Gladys continues. "But the really strange part is the stuff in her trunk. She had boxes of literature on black magic, witchcraft, voodoo, and the like. She even had containers of chicken bones, random exotic herbs, old jewelry — both men and women's, little vials of random liquids. Many of them broken in the wreck, but the police took all the rest. There was more stuff too, but I can't recall all of it."

"Wow. That's crazy creepy," Haley says. "How did you guys find out all of this?"

"The police are here all the time after things like car accidents, gunshot victims, and such," Gladys replies. "We get to know some of them pretty well. Officer Jeremy Benton was the first one on the scene after the accident. I won't frighten you with details, but he said that it was one of the tougher situations he's seen. Suffice it to say that boy's injuries were substantial. Poor Jeremy. When he described it to us, he was visibly disturbed. It's just an awful tragedy all around."

With Gladys still pushing the wheelchair behind me, I can't see her, but I can hear her voice quivering.

"That's awful," I say, thinking more about the witchcraft stuff in the trunk than the tragedy of the accident.

My dads' words from my dream come back to me. He had said, "*That woman is a witch.*"

Haley walks back around to Gladys and gives her a hug.

"What were their names?" I ask, remembering that the names I gave them in my dream where actually not their names, but rather random names I must have picked from my own subconscious. Just as the the elevator reaches the ground floor, the overhead paging system interrupts.

"Gladys Freemont, please contact your nurse's station."

"So sorry, folks. Hang on one second. Can you take the wheel for one-minute, sweetie? Stay here and I'll be right back." Gladys hands the reigns of my wheelchair over to Haley and ducks around a corner.

"It's a trick. Let's make a run for it," Haley jokes, but having been through so much, it scares me just the same.

Just as I'm starting to get genuinely worried, Gladys comes back around the corner, carrying a purse.

"You're probably going to need this." She hands it to Haley.

"Oh, goodness. Where is my brain at?" Haley exclaims. Taking her purse and letting Gladys step back behind the wheelchair.

"With your husband, as it should be." Gladys pleasantly replies.

We push down the hall through a couple of double doors. Daylight streams in through the glass walls of the hospital lobby.

"You were telling me about the people in the accident I say. "What happened to the lady? Is she okay?" I ask.

Gladys pushes me out through the front doors. The fresh air outside has an unexpected chill, but I love it. It's real. As we get closer to the walkway, Gladys continues.

"She was hurt pretty bad in the wreck. She was in a coma too. She held on for a long time. It's such a sad situation. We deal with a lot in this job, and we do our best to put things behind us when we can and focus on saving people. But, we've all been talking about her ever since you woke up. Sometimes really strange coincidences do happen."

Digging through her purse, Haley asks, "Coincidences like what?"

Gladys continues, "Well, she passed away too."

"Oh, that's horrible!" Haley says.

"Yes, truly a senseless tragedy," Gladys replies.

"I'll be right back; I've got to go get the car." Haley walks ahead, out into the parking lot.

Still talking to me, Gladys says, "What makes it even worse is that since they have no next of kin, the state will end up taking care of the burials. They won't have a service, which breaks my heart. Especially for that little boy. So young," Gladys says.

I can tell that Gladys is a kind soul, her eyes mist up a bit talking about them. Looking out to the parking lot, I see Haley pulling up in a grey sedan. I'm guessing it's a rental.

"Anyway, if you and Haley are interested, some of the other hospital staff and I are going to do a little service for them next Wednesday at seven in the evening, in the park adjacent to the hospital. No more than twenty minutes. That poor boy was so young, and his mother so obviously needed spiritual guidance. We'll say a few words and light candles. It just feels right," Gladys says.

"Yeah..." My mind remembering random parts of the dream, making me a little uneasy about going to the service. But dreams are dreams, and I, too, feel sad for them, especially the boy. Gladys is still looking at me, waiting for me to finish my sentence.

"Yes. Of course. We'll be there," I say.

"Well, thank you. You and Haley are good-hearted people. I can tell." Gladys smiles.

"You never did tell me her name," I add.

"Oh, sorry. Her name was Lisa Symmes. Her son was Tyler," she replies.

I'm in shock for a moment, knowing that no one ever told me their names. How could I have guessed that in my dream? Did someone say their names in my hospital room? Haley didn't even know their names.

Haley pulls up and Gladys helps me stand as Haley walks around the front of the car to assist me in getting in.

"I'm fine, really," I say, sitting down in the passenger seat.

Haley gives Gladys a big hug and they both seem on the verge of tears again.

"Steve I and were talking about the service we are planning for next week. He said you guys would be okay to come to a simple service next week for the woman and her son from the accident," Gladys says. "You good with that?"

"Oh, of course!" Haley says. "We'll see you then, and thank you so much for everything. We'll stay in touch. I promise," Haley says, wiping her eyes.

"I hope so. You two are a pleasure and I wish you both a speedy recovery together," Gladys smiles at us both. Her yellow, crooked-tooth smile now warm and comforting.

I can't think of any plausible way that I'd know their names, and as Haley shuts my door and comes around to the driver's seat, I roll my window down.

"Thank you, Gladys!" I say, my voice still too weak to yell.

"I'll see you guys next week!" She reminds us, as Haley starts to pull away.

"Wait." I say, and she turns back around to face us. "What is it?" Gladys asks.

"What was the coincidence?" I ask. "You said that sometimes really strong coincidences occur."

"Oh..." Gladys pauses. "The woman, Lisa, her passing was literally seconds before we heard Haley screaming in excitement about you waking up. Steve, you two were in a coma for almost six weeks to the day, and almost exactly the same amount of time."

"Wow, that is a coincidence, and kind of creepy," Haley says, pulling the car away from the hospital.

As we pull away, a vision pops up in my head. The construction site. In an instant, I remember Lisa chasing me with an ax, and then falling. Lisa hitting the ground seconds before I... before I woke up.

Suddenly, my body is instantly covered in goosebumps. Sitting here in this rental car, next to the love of my life, my mind fills with endless questions for a moment. As I reach for the answers in my mind; answers to these seemingly impossible happenings, my thoughts return to the inky black depths from which I emerged.

It's in that exact moment that I come to a great realization. No one will ever believe me, not even Haley. I don't blame her. It seems impossible. It probably is impossible. But, I know what really happened to me. I know what I have really endured over the past six weeks. It is something I will have to keep to myself for the rest of my life, lest people think I am crazy. So, I will. I'll keep this secret here. Just between Lisa, Tyler and me.

Here, in the dark.

ALSO BY DANIEL FOX

Lies That Bind

In those small spaces between the mundane day-to-day tasks. That's where most people make real connections with each other.

But ...I'm only repeating what I've heard. I'm not allowed to make those connections. I can't afford to take those risks. Those are the rules.

Soon, we will have to run again. To lie again.

We will have to go on pretending.

The madman is coming. He is violent and deranged. A killer on the hunt, and he always finds us. No matter how far we go, or how well we hide. It's almost as if he has some supernatural ability to track us down.

I've always kept my head down, followed the plan. I've done whatever it takes to protect my parents. To save my family. But this time it's different. I broke the rules, and now I don't want to let her go. I want to stay here and live my life, like a normal person.

I can't take this anymore.

The only way to end the cycle is to stop the madman.

So that's what I'm going to do.

CPSIA information can be obtained
at www.ICGtesting.com
Printed in the USA
LVHW081952170220
647200LV00026B/736

9 780578 632346